SUMMER CAMP
SCIENCE
MYSTERIES

#8 **The Yucky Duck Rescue**

A Mystery about Pollution

by Lynda Beauregard
illustrated by German Torres

GRAPHIC UNIVERSE™ • MINNEAPOLIS • NEW YORK

W

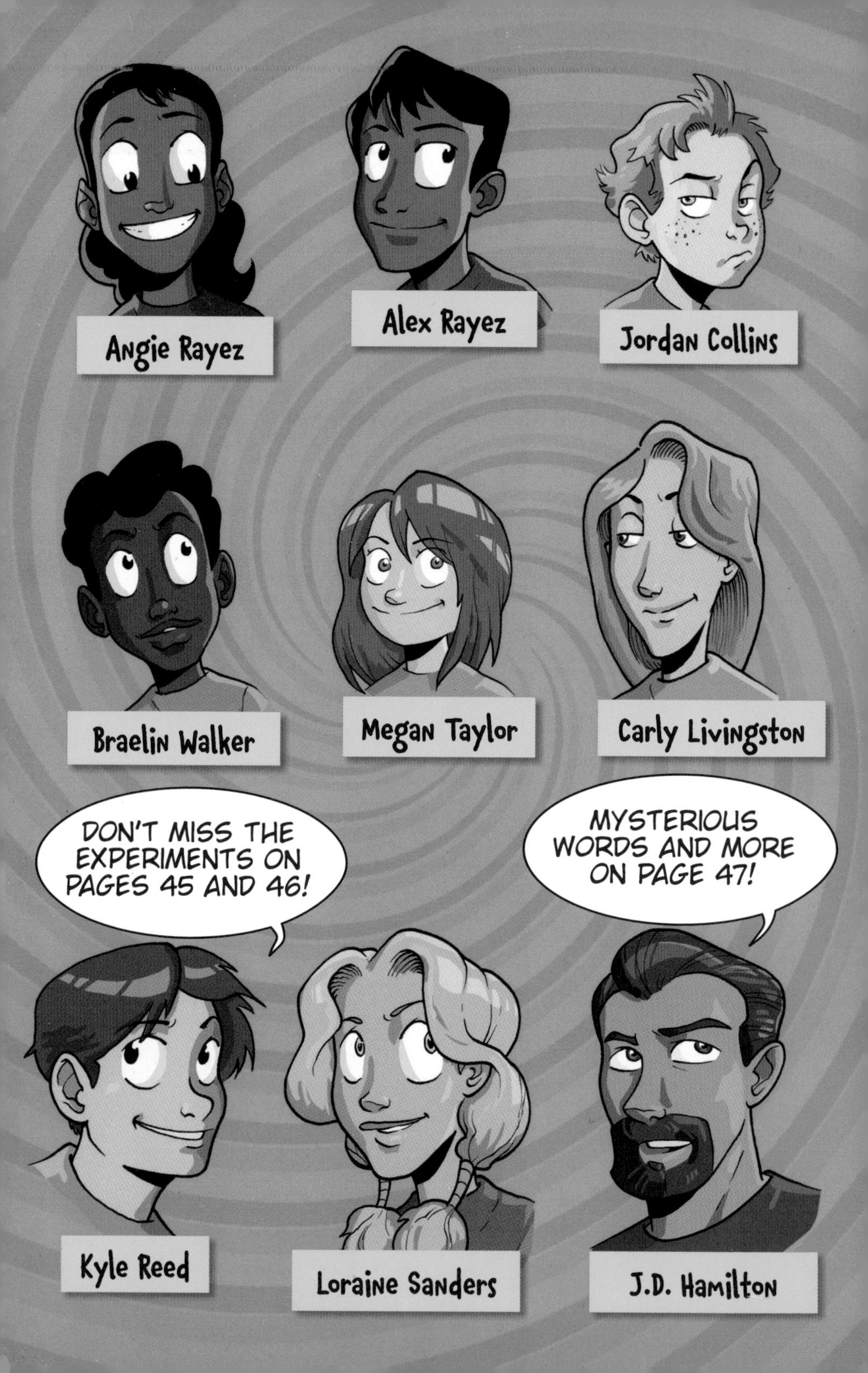
Angie Rayez
Alex Rayez
Jordan Collins
Braelin Walker
Megan Taylor
Carly Livingston
DON'T MISS THE EXPERIMENTS ON PAGES 45 AND 46!
MYSTERIOUS WORDS AND MORE ON PAGE 47!
Kyle Reed
Loraine Sanders
J.D. Hamilton

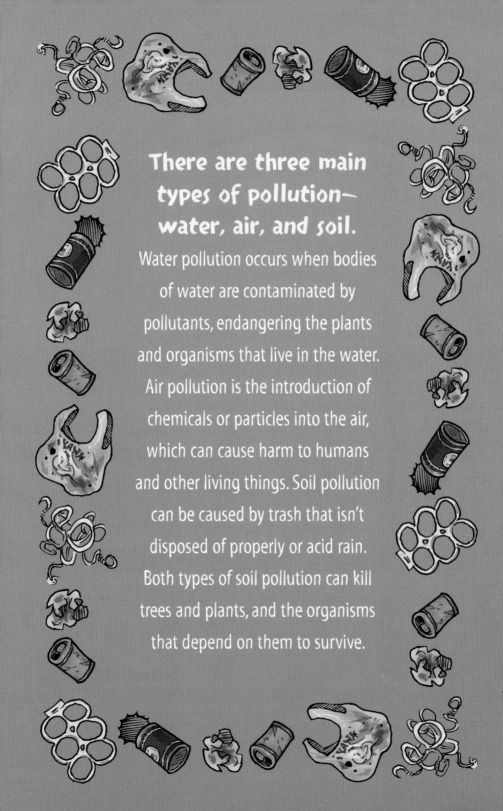

# There are three main types of pollution—water, air, and soil.

Water pollution occurs when bodies of water are contaminated by pollutants, endangering the plants and organisms that live in the water. Air pollution is the introduction of chemicals or particles into the air, which can cause harm to humans and other living things. Soil pollution can be caused by trash that isn't disposed of properly or acid rain. Both types of soil pollution can kill trees and plants, and the organisms that depend on them to survive.

Story by Lynda Beauregard

Art by German Torres

Coloring by Pat Barrett

Lettering by Grace Lu

Graphic Universe™
A division of Lerner Publishing Group, Inc.
241 First Avenue North
Minneapolis, MN 55401 U.S.A.

Website address: www.lernerbooks.com

Main body text set in CCWildwords.
Typeface provided by Comicraft/Active Images.

Library of Congress Cataloging-in-Publication Data

Beauregard, Lynda.

The yucky duck rescue : a mystery about pollution / by Lynda Beauregard ; illustrated by German Torres.

p. cm. — (Summer camp science mysteries ; #8)

Summary: "The campers solve a mystery centered on the effects of pollution on the environment." — Provided by the publisher.

ISBN 978-1-4677-0170-9 (lib. bdg. : alk. paper)

1. Graphic novels. [1. Graphic novels. 2. Camps—Fiction. 3. Pollution—Fiction. 4. Environmentalism—Fiction.] I. Torres, German, ill. II. Title.

PZ7.7.B42Yuc 2013

741.5'973—dc23                                              2012030912

Manufactured in the United States of America
1 – CG – 12/31/12

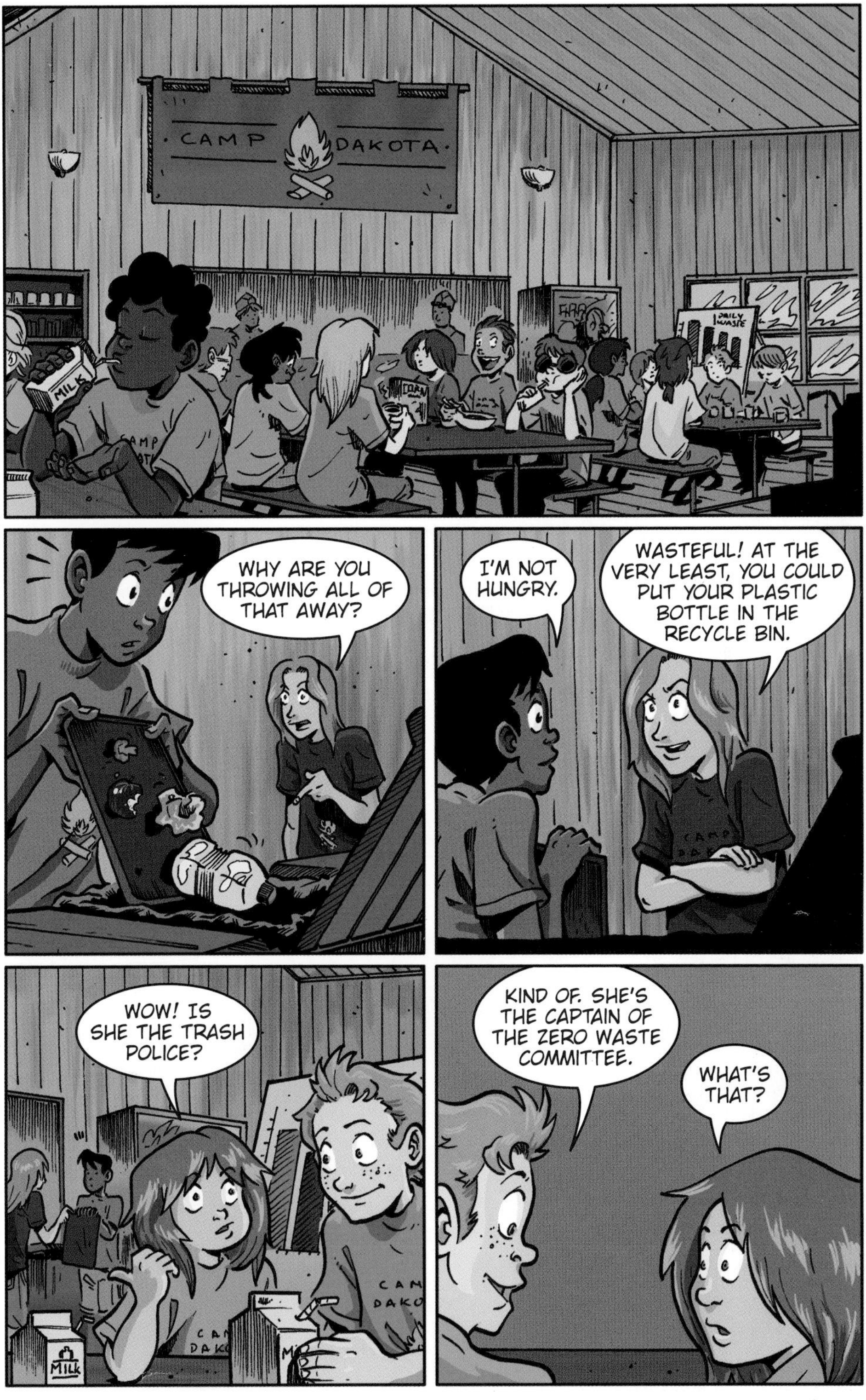
CAMP DAKOTA
MILK
CORN
DAILY WASTE
WHY ARE YOU THROWING ALL OF THAT AWAY?
I'M NOT HUNGRY.
WASTEFUL! AT THE VERY LEAST, YOU COULD PUT YOUR PLASTIC BOTTLE IN THE RECYCLE BIN.
WOW! IS SHE THE TRASH POLICE?
KIND OF. SHE'S THE CAPTAIN OF THE ZERO WASTE COMMITTEE.
WHAT'S THAT?
MILK

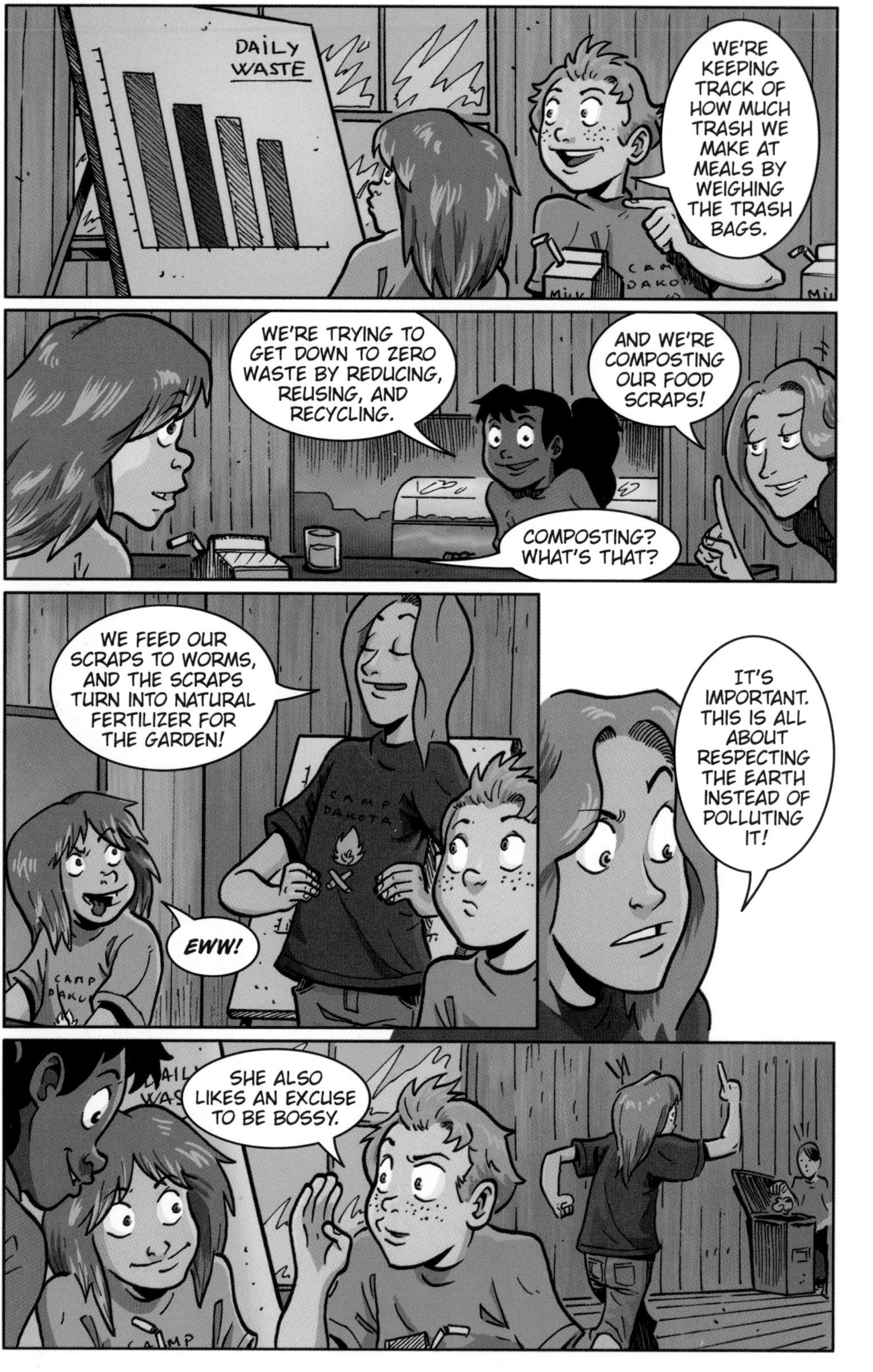
DAILY WASTE
WE'RE KEEPING TRACK OF HOW MUCH TRASH WE MAKE AT MEALS BY WEIGHING THE TRASH BAGS.
WE'RE TRYING TO GET DOWN TO ZERO WASTE BY REDUCING, REUSING, AND RECYCLING.
AND WE'RE COMPOSTING OUR FOOD SCRAPS!
COMPOSTING? WHAT'S THAT?
WE FEED OUR SCRAPS TO WORMS, AND THE SCRAPS TURN INTO NATURAL FERTILIZER FOR THE GARDEN!
EWW!
IT'S IMPORTANT. THIS IS ALL ABOUT RESPECTING THE EARTH INSTEAD OF POLLUTING IT!
SHE ALSO LIKES AN EXCUSE TO BE BOSSY.

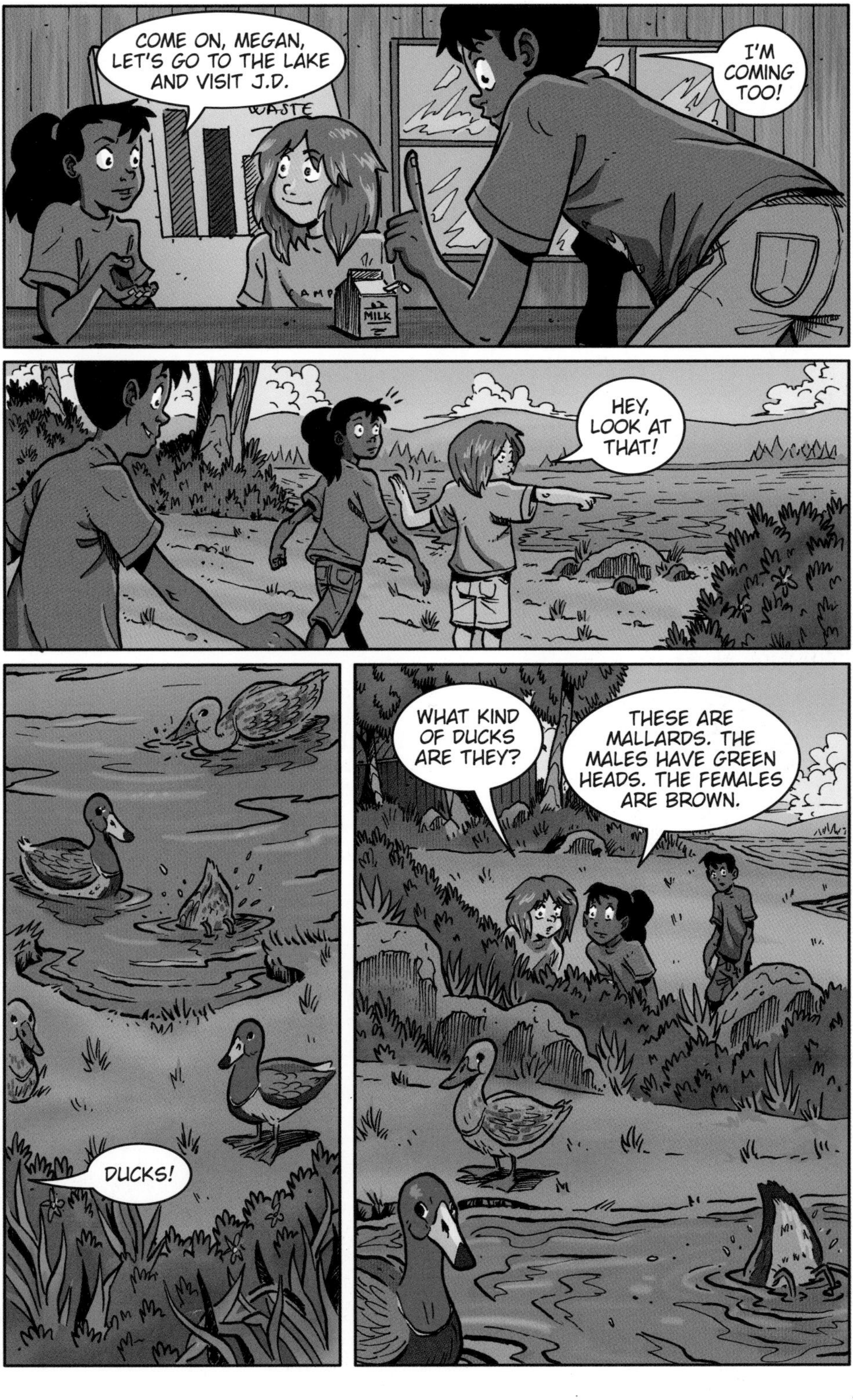
COME ON, MEGAN, LET'S GO TO THE LAKE AND VISIT J.D.
I'M COMING TOO!
MILK
HEY, LOOK AT THAT!
DUCKS!
WHAT KIND OF DUCKS ARE THEY?
THESE ARE MALLARDS. THE MALES HAVE GREEN HEADS. THE FEMALES ARE BROWN.

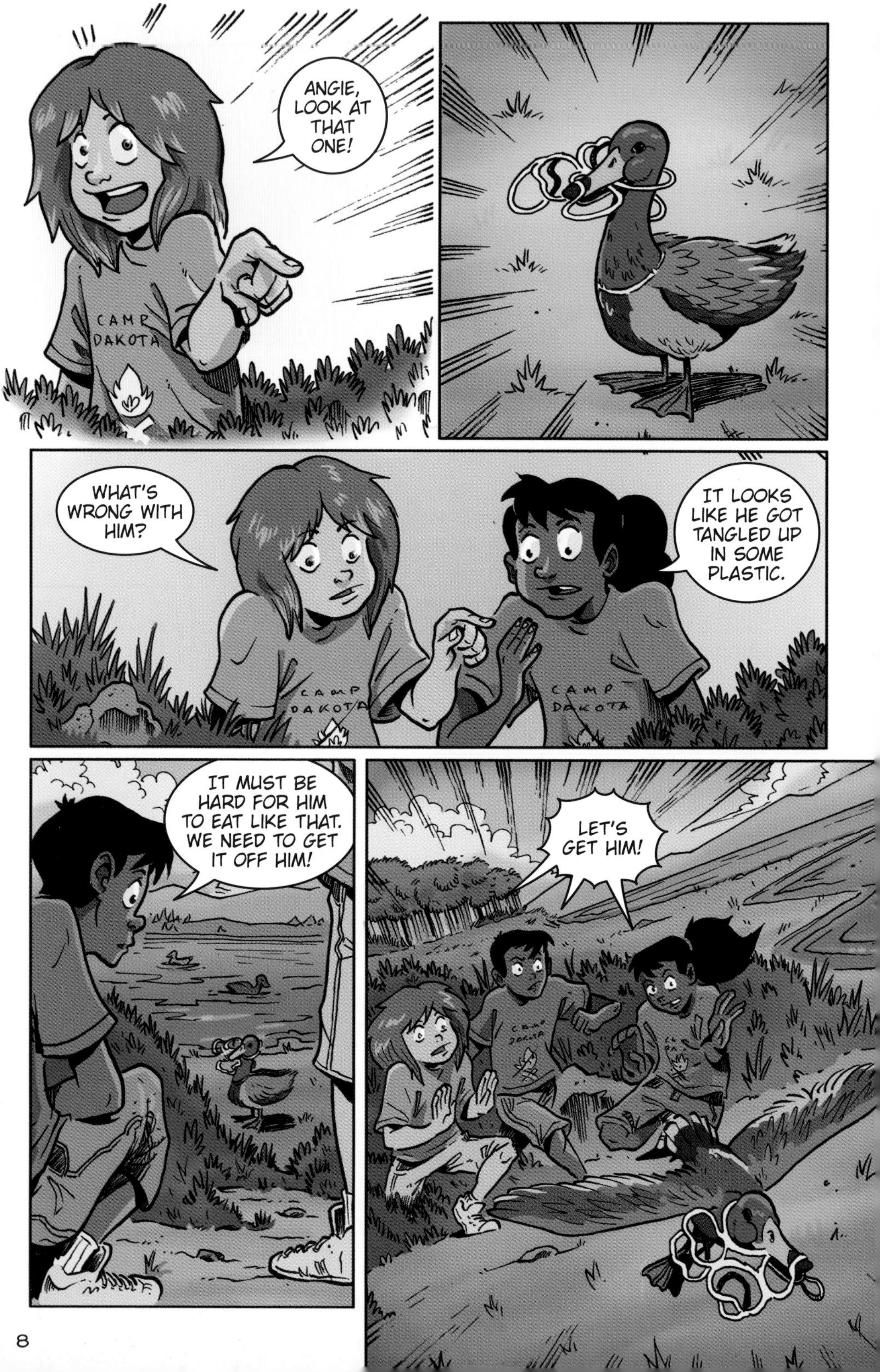
ANGIE, LOOK AT THAT ONE!
CAMP DAKOTA
WHAT'S WRONG WITH HIM?
IT LOOKS LIKE HE GOT TANGLED UP IN SOME PLASTIC.
IT MUST BE HARD FOR HIM TO EAT LIKE THAT. WE NEED TO GET IT OFF HIM!
LET'S GET HIM!

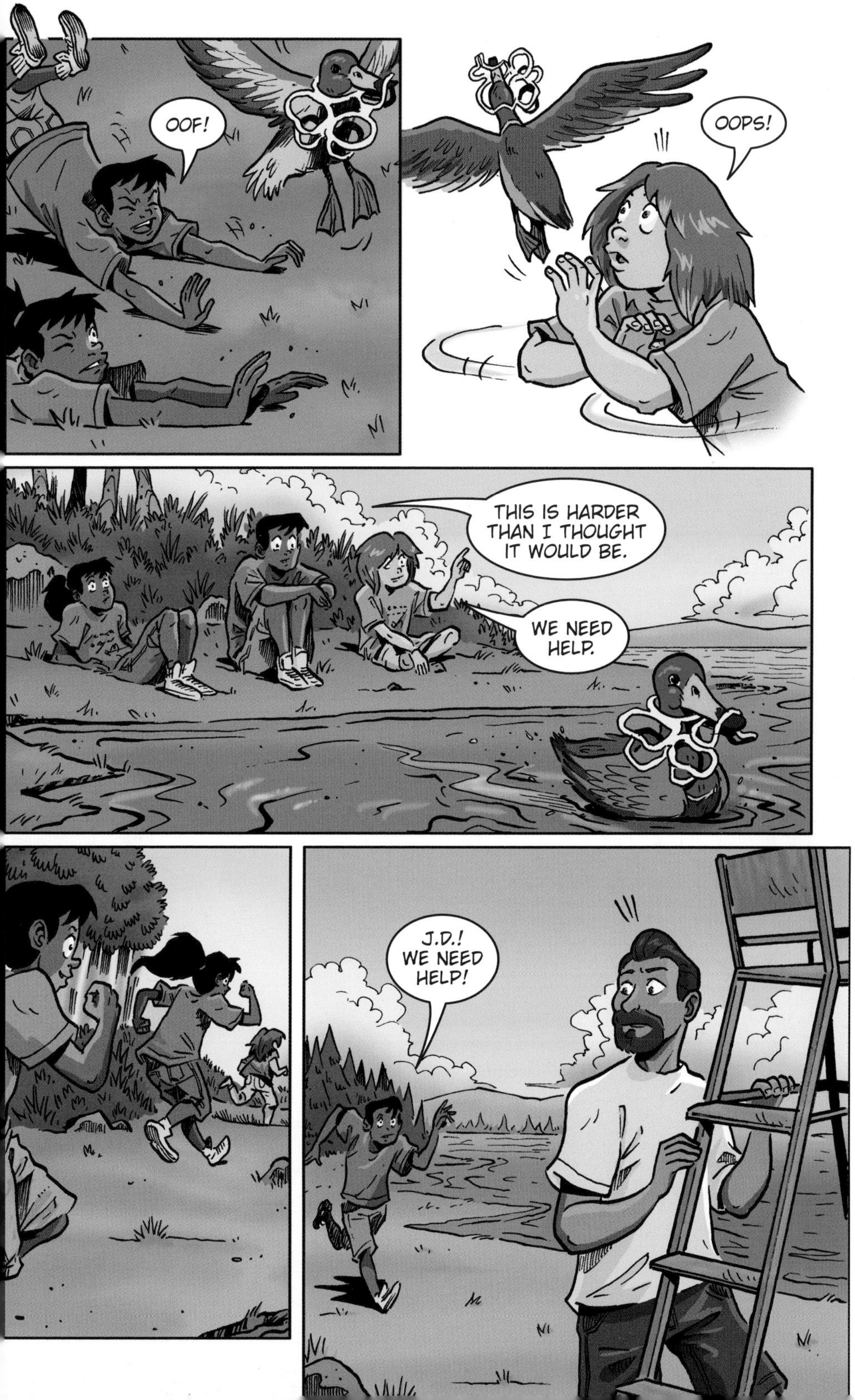
OOF!
OOPS!
THIS IS HARDER THAN I THOUGHT IT WOULD BE.
WE NEED HELP.
J.D.! WE NEED HELP!

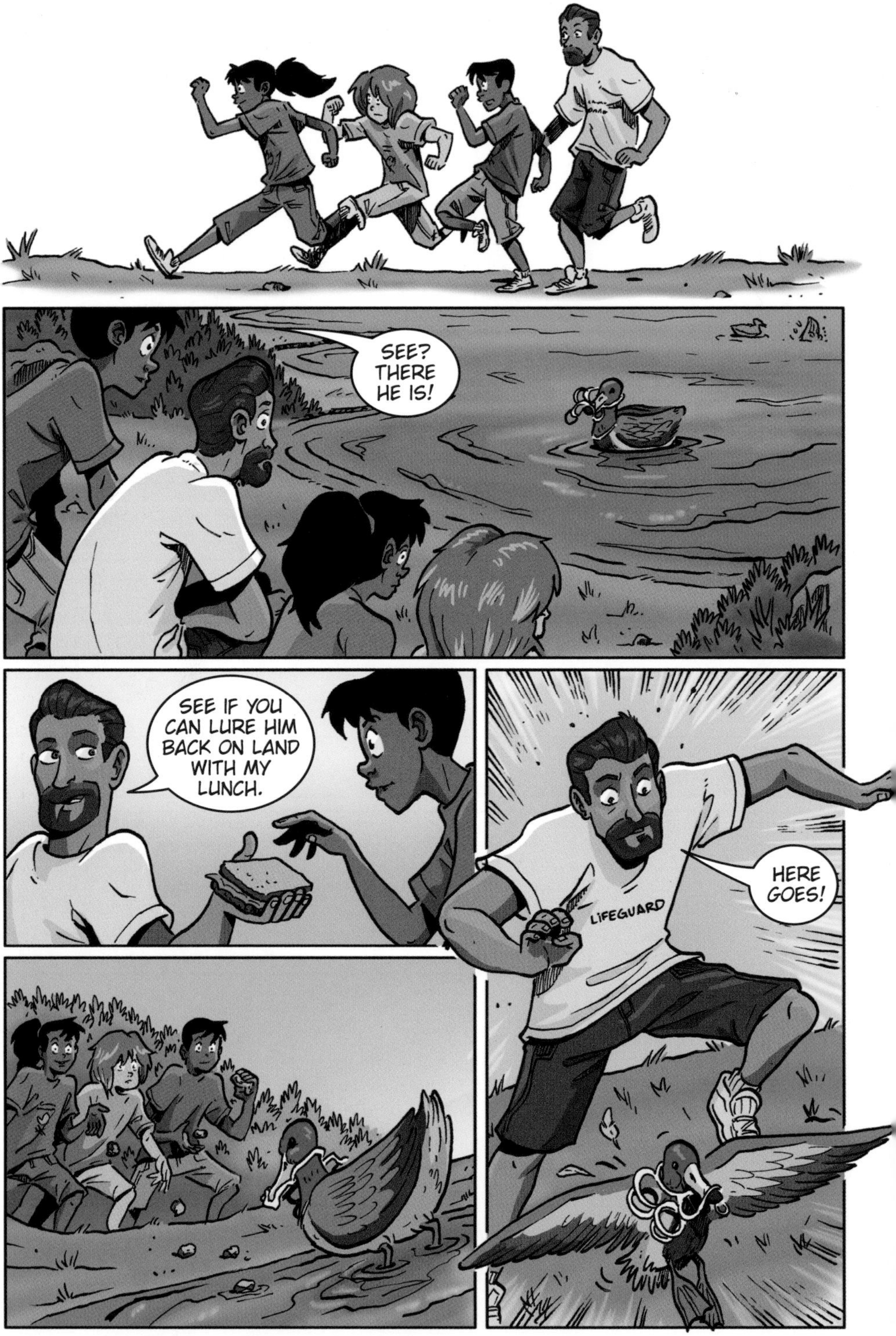
SEE? THERE HE IS!
SEE IF YOU CAN LURE HIM BACK ON LAND WITH MY LUNCH.
HERE GOES!
LIFEGUARD

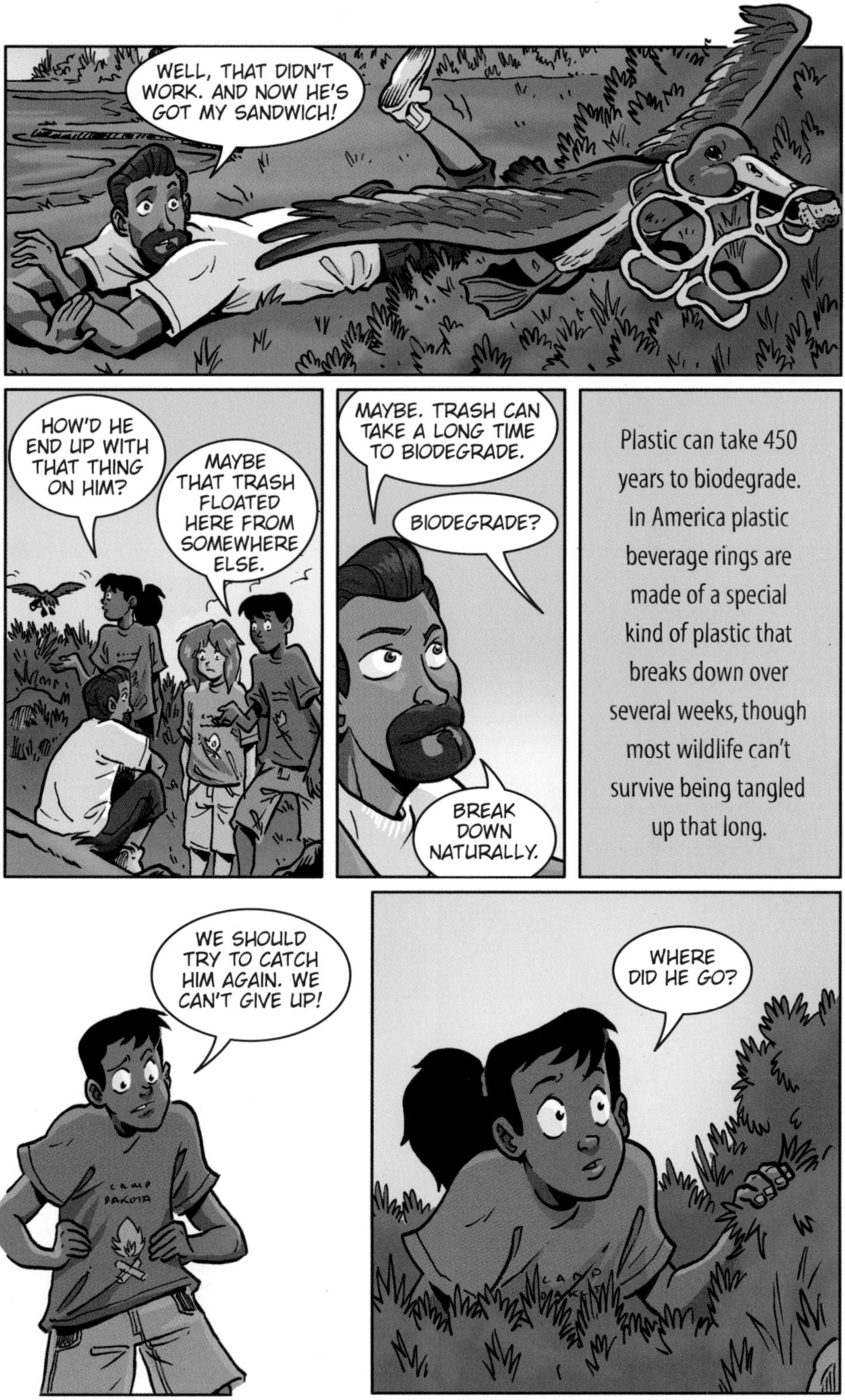
WELL, THAT DIDN'T WORK. AND NOW HE'S GOT MY SANDWICH!
HOW'D HE END UP WITH THAT THING ON HIM?
MAYBE THAT TRASH FLOATED HERE FROM SOMEWHERE ELSE.
MAYBE. TRASH CAN TAKE A LONG TIME TO BIODEGRADE.
BIODEGRADE?
BREAK DOWN NATURALLY.
Plastic can take 450 years to biodegrade. In America plastic beverage rings are made of a special kind of plastic that breaks down over several weeks, though most wildlife can't survive being tangled up that long.
WE SHOULD TRY TO CATCH HIM AGAIN. WE CAN'T GIVE UP!
WHERE DID HE GO?

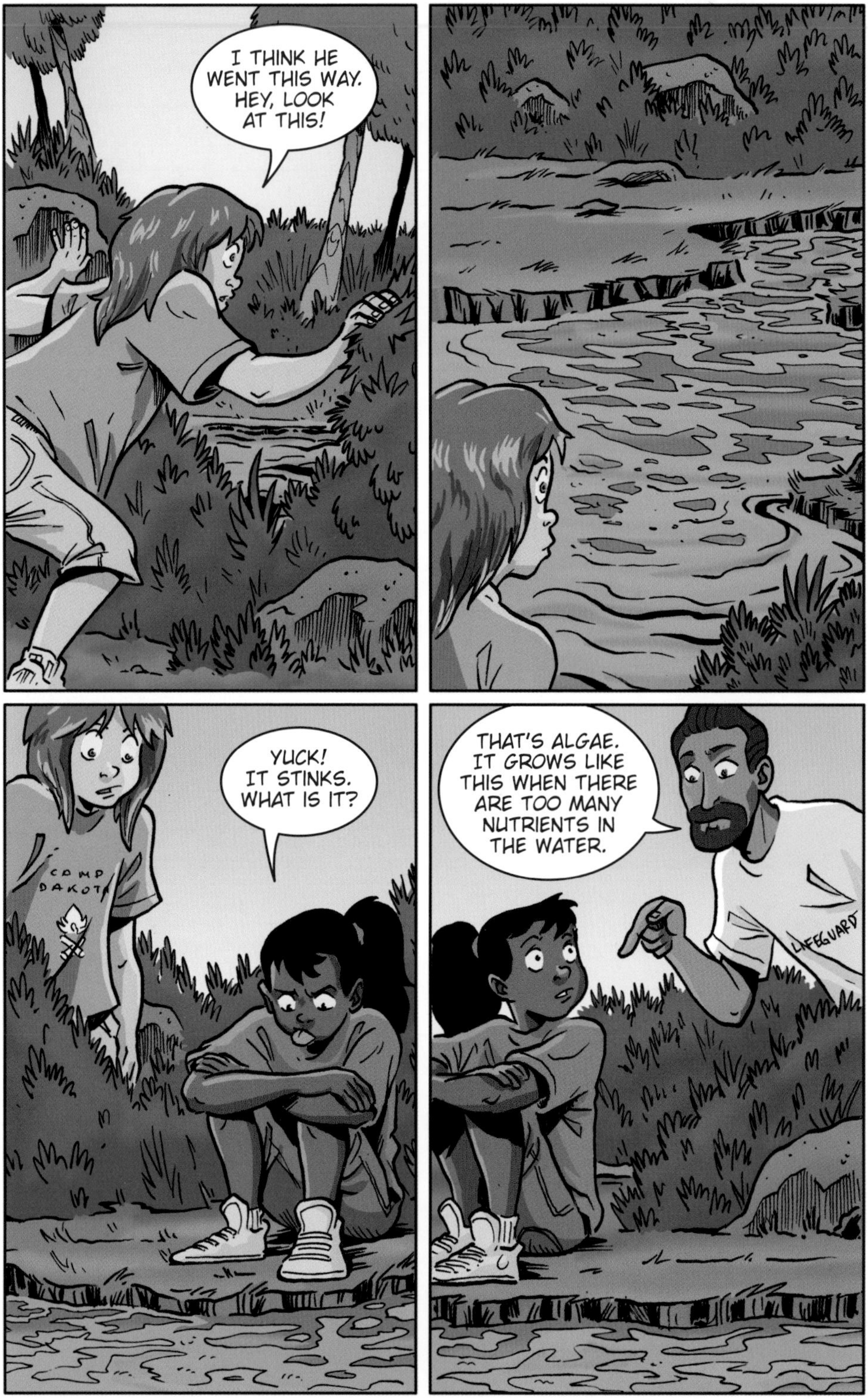
I THINK HE WENT THIS WAY. HEY, LOOK AT THIS!
YUCK! IT STINKS. WHAT IS IT?
THAT'S ALGAE. IT GROWS LIKE THIS WHEN THERE ARE TOO MANY NUTRIENTS IN THE WATER.
LIFEGUARD

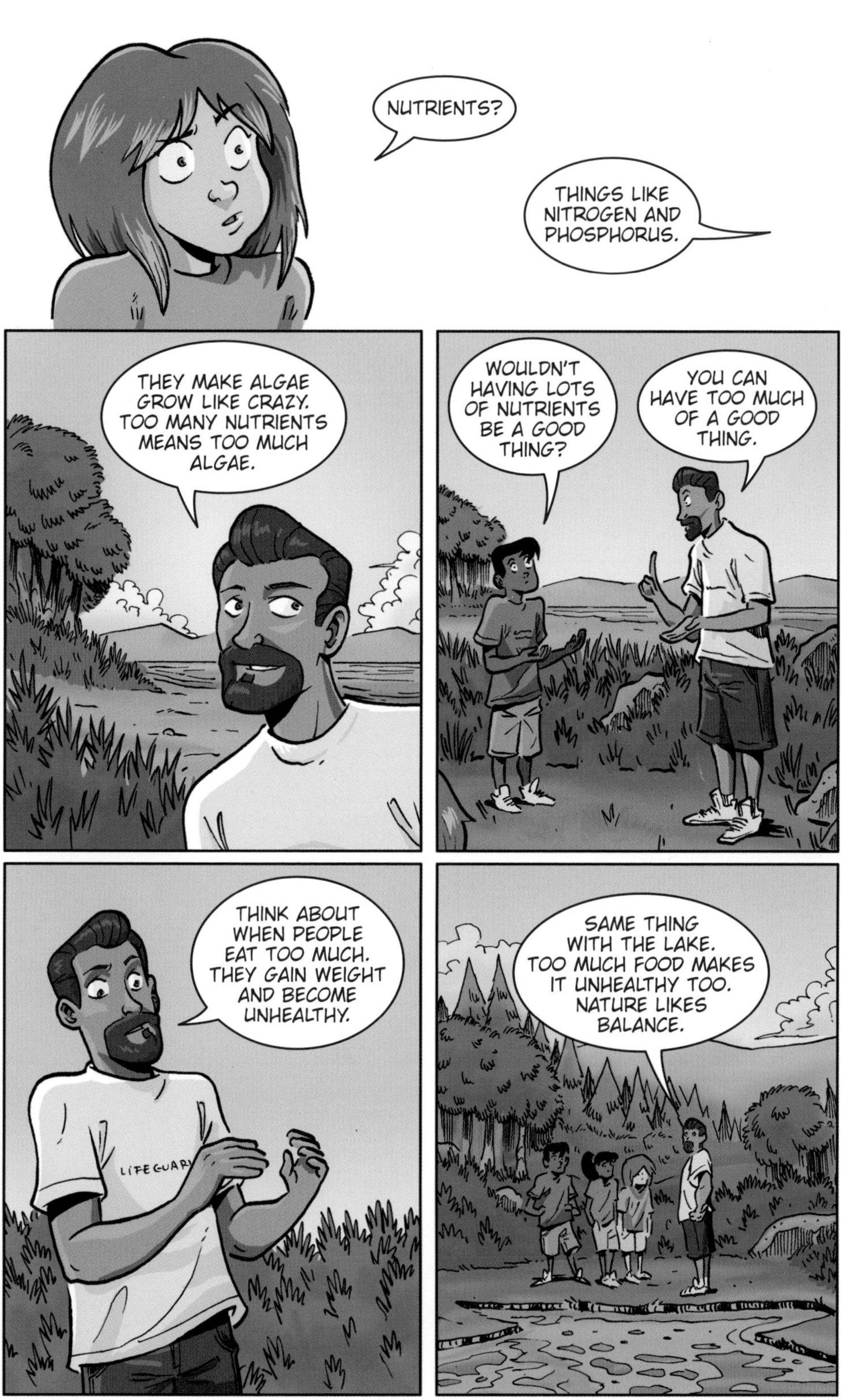
NUTRIENTS?
THINGS LIKE NITROGEN AND PHOSPHORUS.
THEY MAKE ALGAE GROW LIKE CRAZY. TOO MANY NUTRIENTS MEANS TOO MUCH ALGAE.
WOULDN'T HAVING LOTS OF NUTRIENTS BE A GOOD THING?
YOU CAN HAVE TOO MUCH OF A GOOD THING.
THINK ABOUT WHEN PEOPLE EAT TOO MUCH. THEY GAIN WEIGHT AND BECOME UNHEALTHY.
LIFEGUAR
SAME THING WITH THE LAKE. TOO MUCH FOOD MAKES IT UNHEALTHY TOO. NATURE LIKES BALANCE.

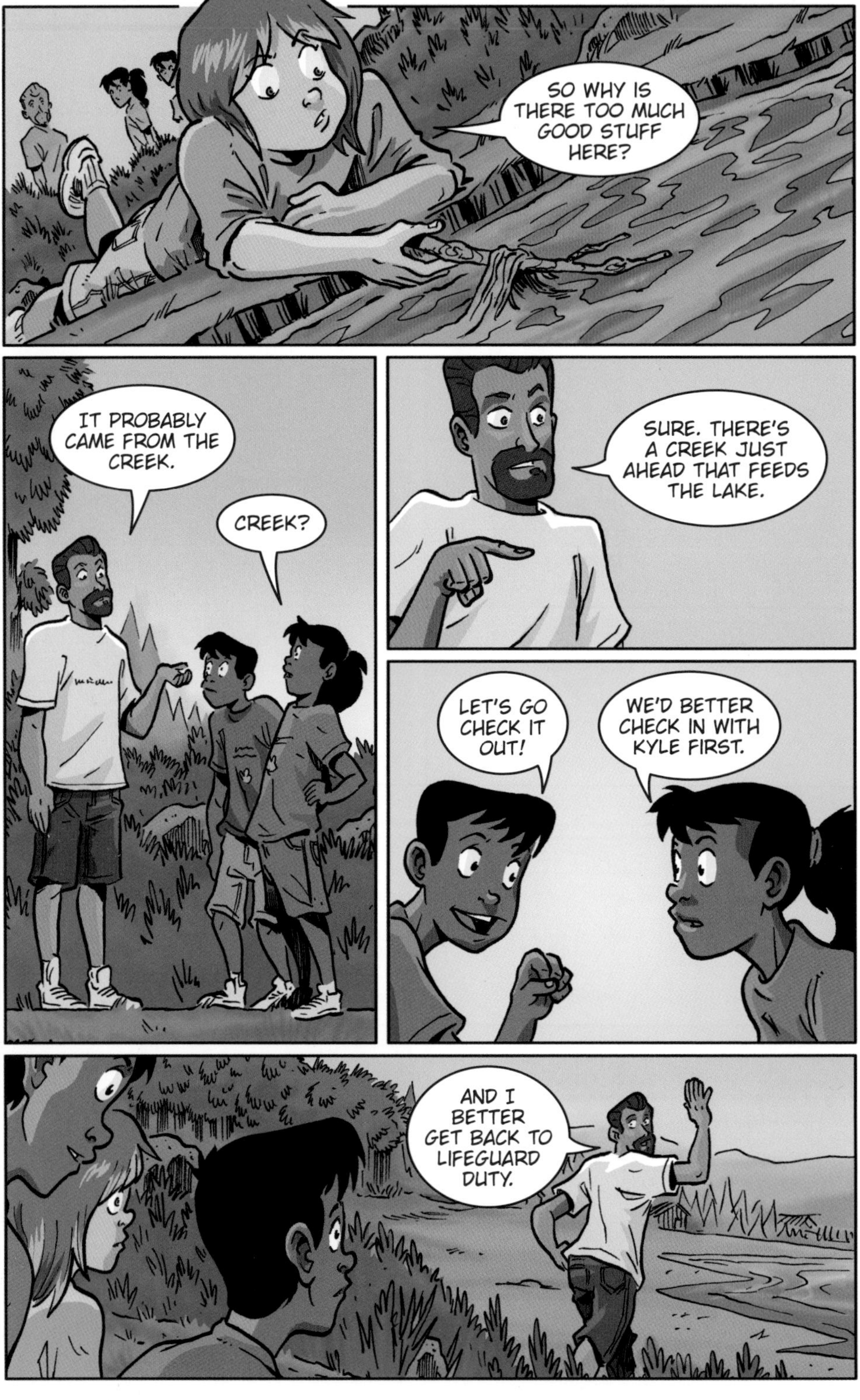
SO WHY IS THERE TOO MUCH GOOD STUFF HERE?
IT PROBABLY CAME FROM THE CREEK.
CREEK?
SURE. THERE'S A CREEK JUST AHEAD THAT FEEDS THE LAKE.
LET'S GO CHECK IT OUT!
WE'D BETTER CHECK IN WITH KYLE FIRST.
AND I BETTER GET BACK TO LIFEGUARD DUTY.

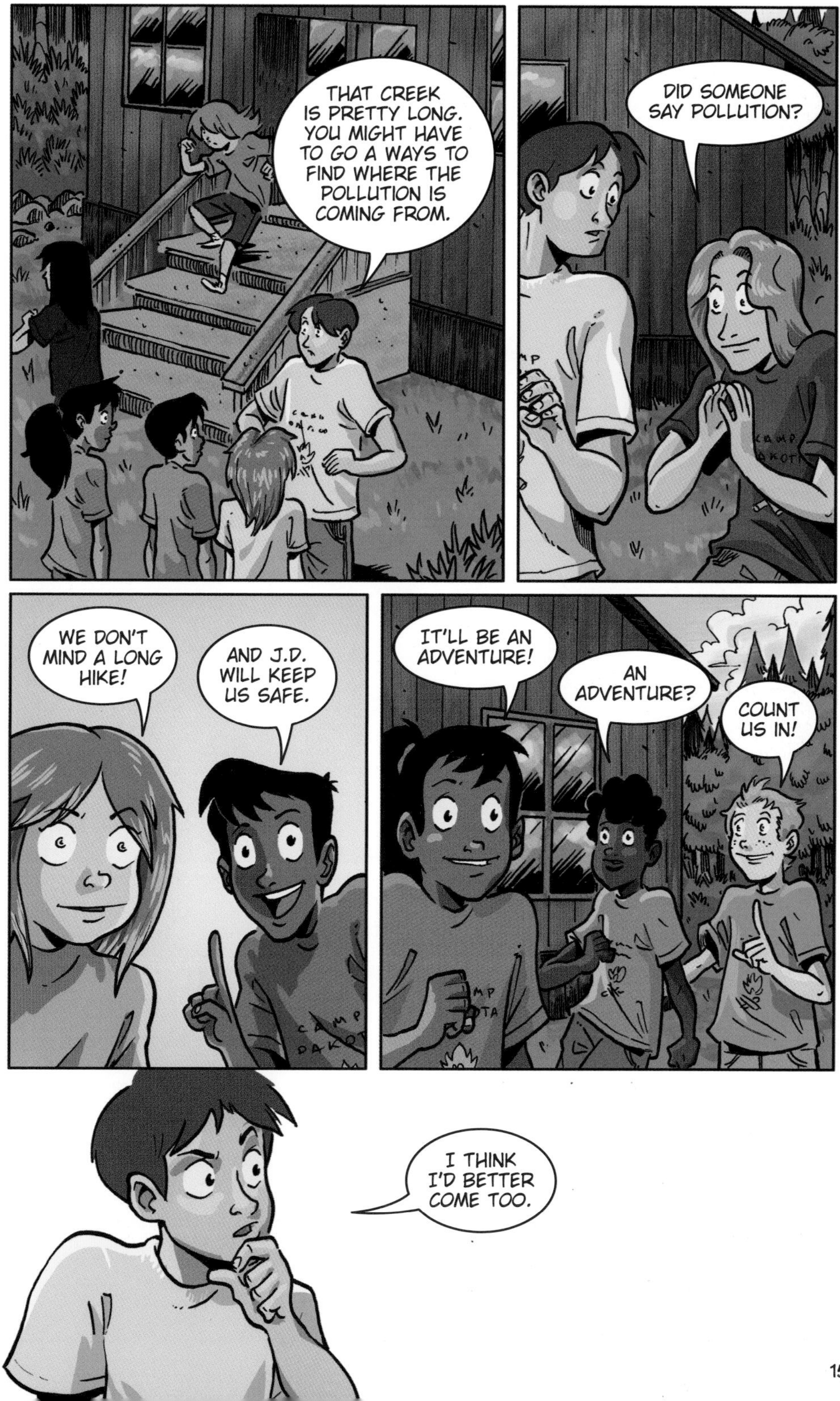
THAT CREEK IS PRETTY LONG. YOU MIGHT HAVE TO GO A WAYS TO FIND WHERE THE POLLUTION IS COMING FROM.
DID SOMEONE SAY POLLUTION?
WE DON'T MIND A LONG HIKE!
AND J.D. WILL KEEP US SAFE.
IT'LL BE AN ADVENTURE!
AN ADVENTURE?
COUNT US IN!
I THINK I'D BETTER COME TOO.

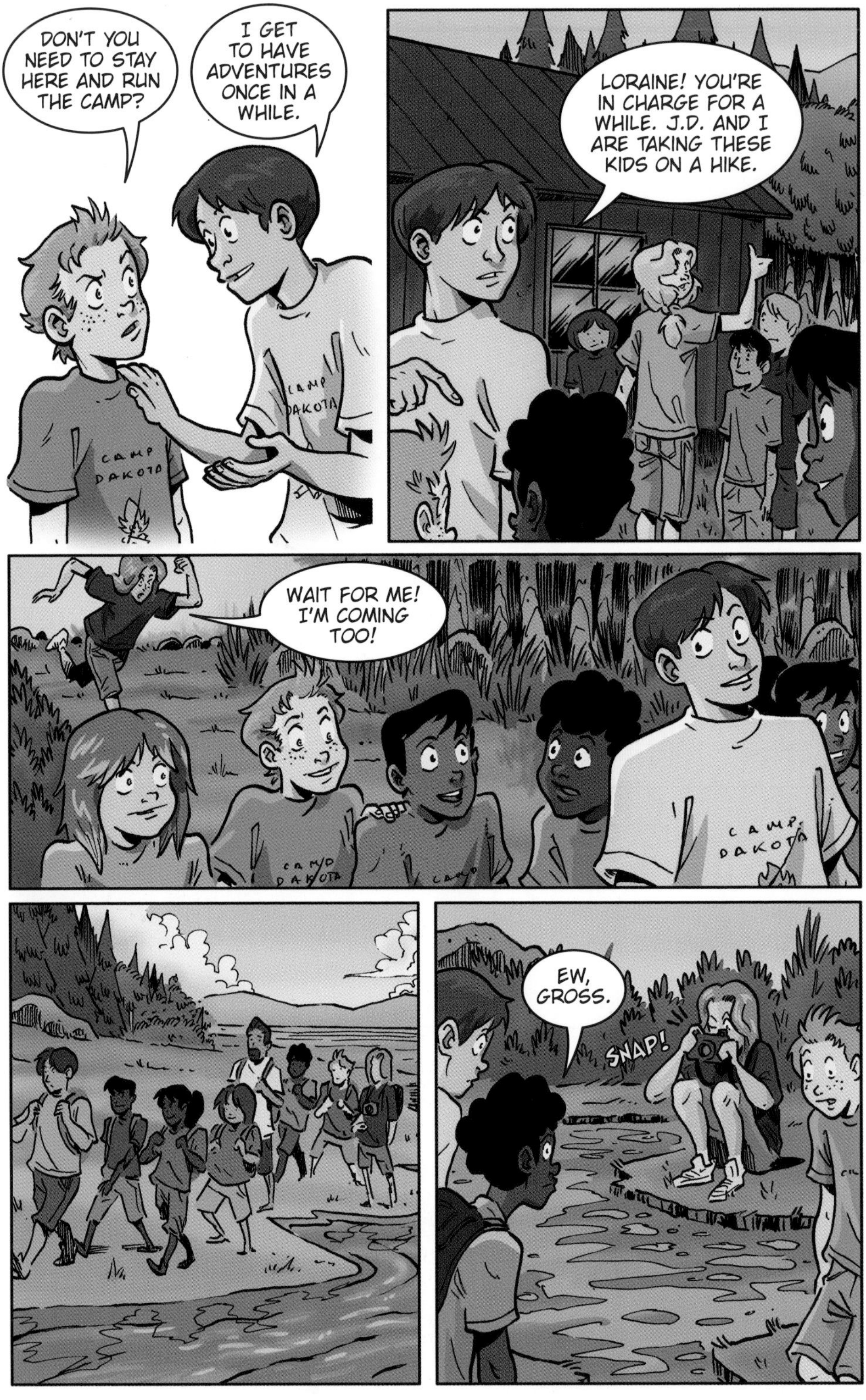
DON'T YOU NEED TO STAY HERE AND RUN THE CAMP?
I GET TO HAVE ADVENTURES ONCE IN A WHILE.
LORAINE! YOU'RE IN CHARGE FOR A WHILE. J.D. AND I ARE TAKING THESE KIDS ON A HIKE.
WAIT FOR ME! I'M COMING TOO!
EW, GROSS.
SNAP!

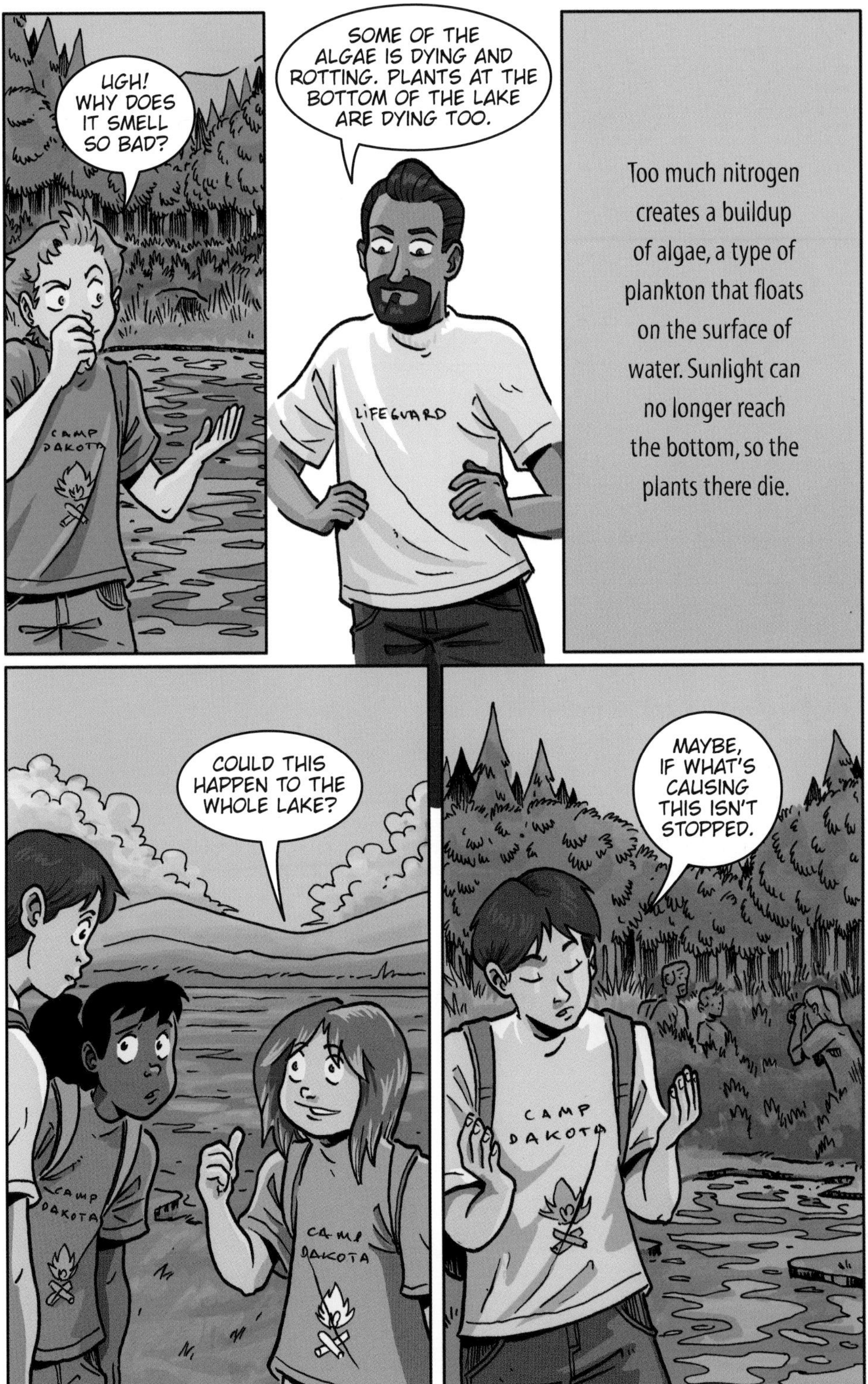
UGH! WHY DOES IT SMELL SO BAD?
CAMP DAKOTA
SOME OF THE ALGAE IS DYING AND ROTTING. PLANTS AT THE BOTTOM OF THE LAKE ARE DYING TOO.
LIFEGUARD
Too much nitrogen creates a buildup of algae, a type of plankton that floats on the surface of water. Sunlight can no longer reach the bottom, so the plants there die.
COULD THIS HAPPEN TO THE WHOLE LAKE?
CAMP DAKOTA
CAMP DAKOTA
MAYBE, IF WHAT'S CAUSING THIS ISN'T STOPPED.
CAMP DAKOTA

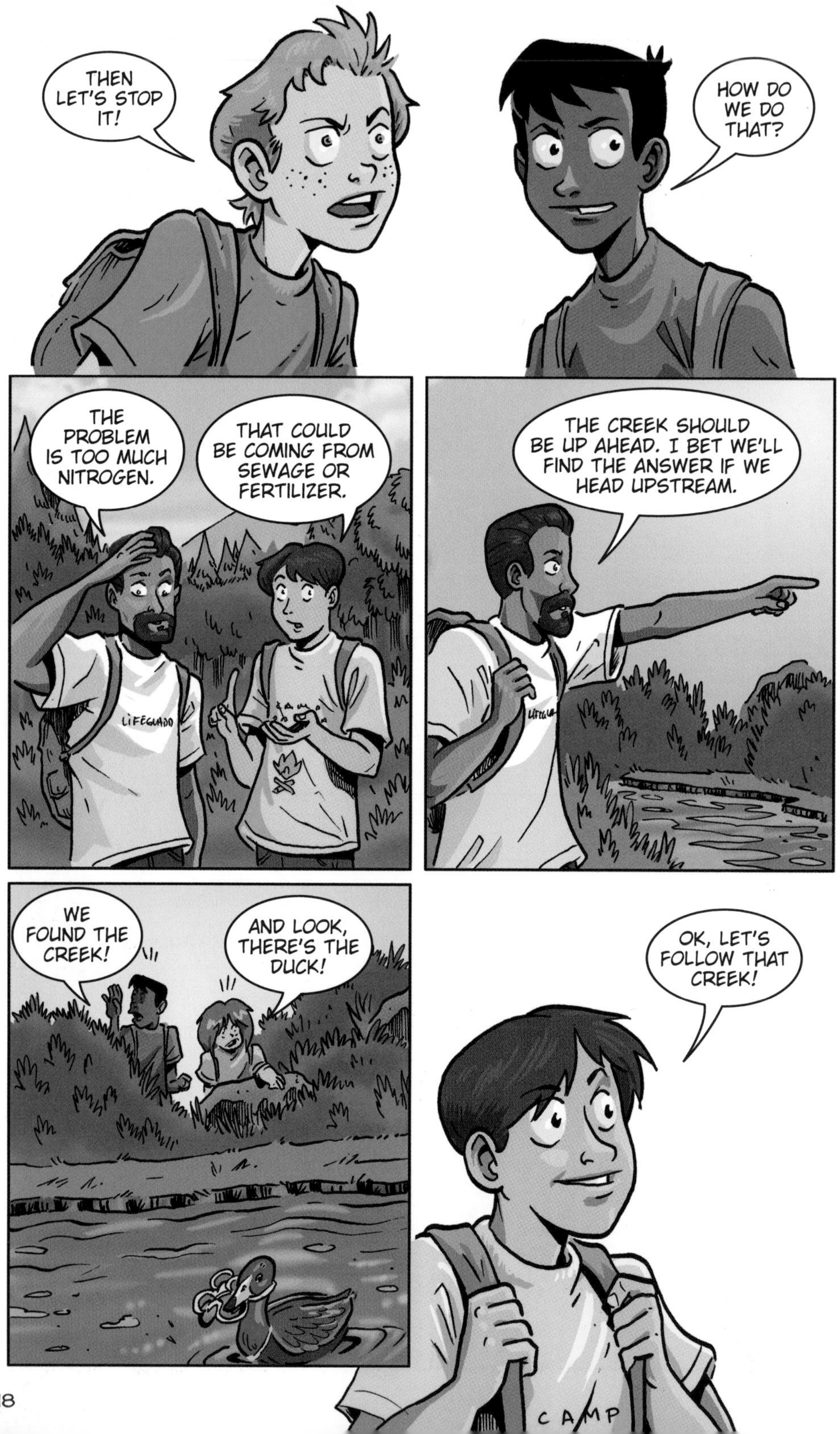
THEN LET'S STOP IT!
HOW DO WE DO THAT?
THE PROBLEM IS TOO MUCH NITROGEN.
THAT COULD BE COMING FROM SEWAGE OR FERTILIZER.
THE CREEK SHOULD BE UP AHEAD. I BET WE'LL FIND THE ANSWER IF WE HEAD UPSTREAM.
WE FOUND THE CREEK!
AND LOOK, THERE'S THE DUCK!
OK, LET'S FOLLOW THAT CREEK!
CAMP

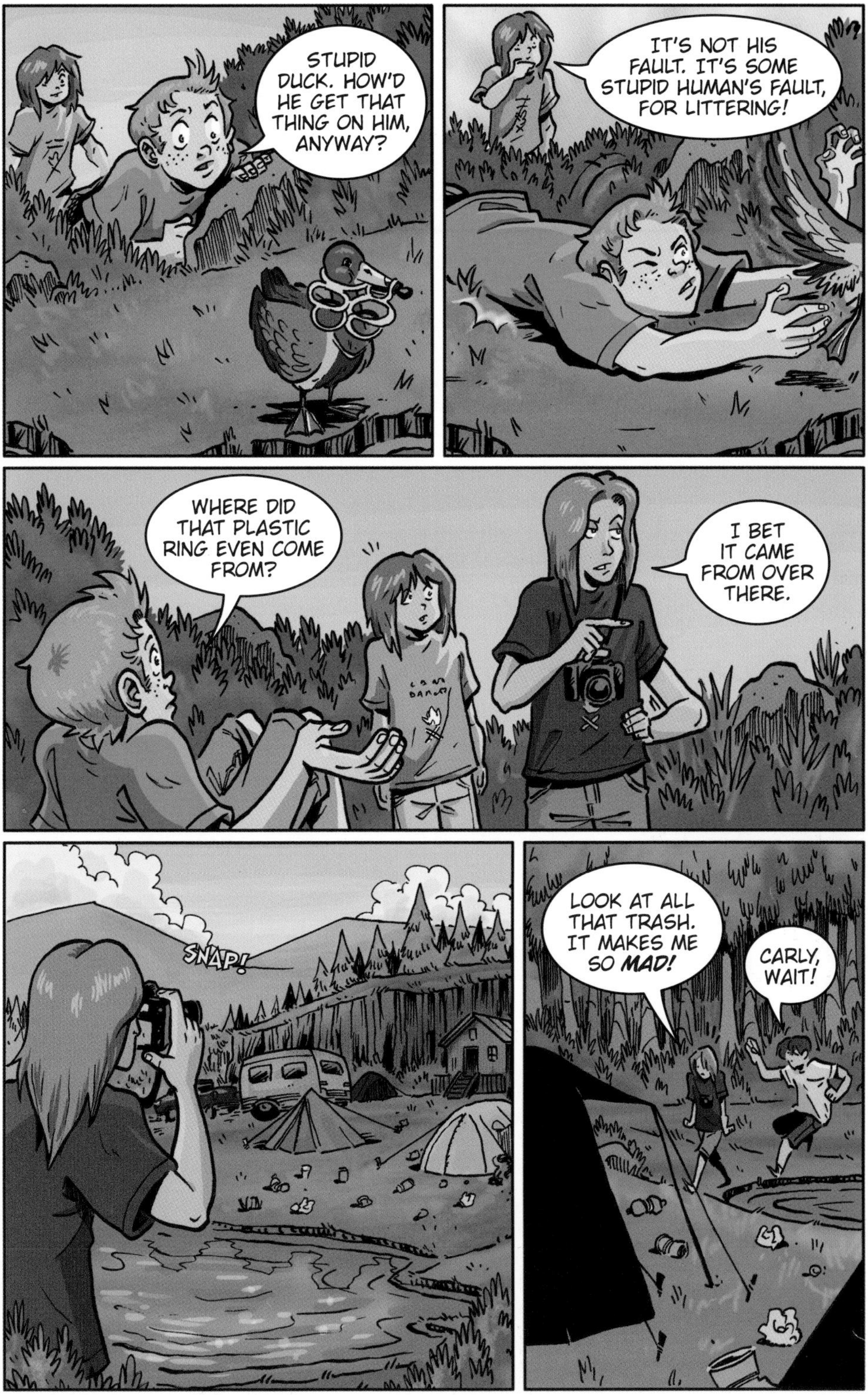
STUPID DUCK. HOW'D HE GET THAT THING ON HIM, ANYWAY?
IT'S NOT HIS FAULT. IT'S SOME STUPID HUMAN'S FAULT, FOR LITTERING!
WHERE DID THAT PLASTIC RING EVEN COME FROM?
I BET IT CAME FROM OVER THERE.
SNAP!
LOOK AT ALL THAT TRASH. IT MAKES ME SO *MAD!*
CARLY, WAIT!

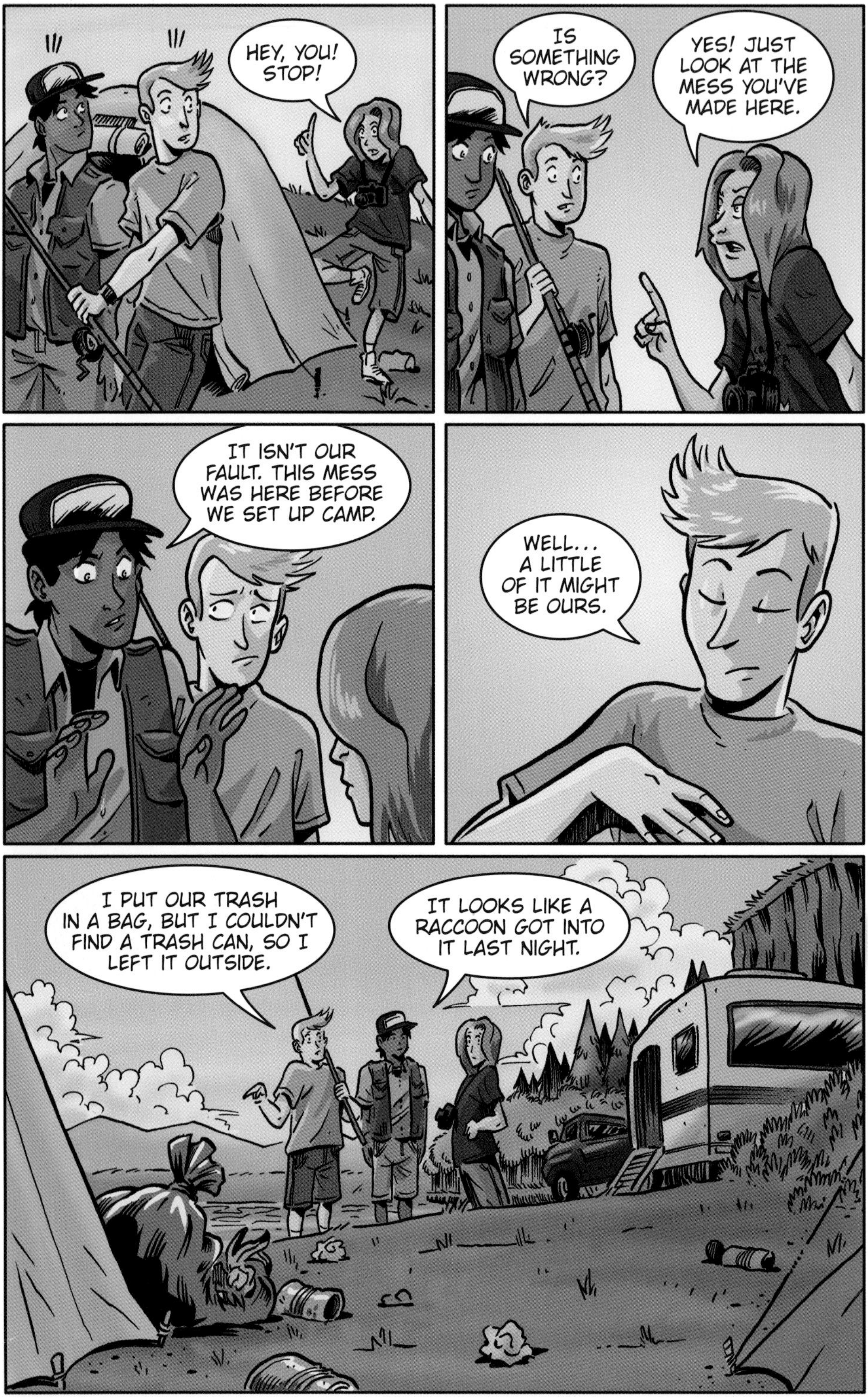
HEY, YOU! STOP!
IS SOMETHING WRONG?
YES! JUST LOOK AT THE MESS YOU'VE MADE HERE.
IT ISN'T OUR FAULT. THIS MESS WAS HERE BEFORE WE SET UP CAMP.
WELL... A LITTLE OF IT MIGHT BE OURS.
I PUT OUR TRASH IN A BAG, BUT I COULDN'T FIND A TRASH CAN, SO I LEFT IT OUTSIDE.
IT LOOKS LIKE A RACCOON GOT INTO IT LAST NIGHT.

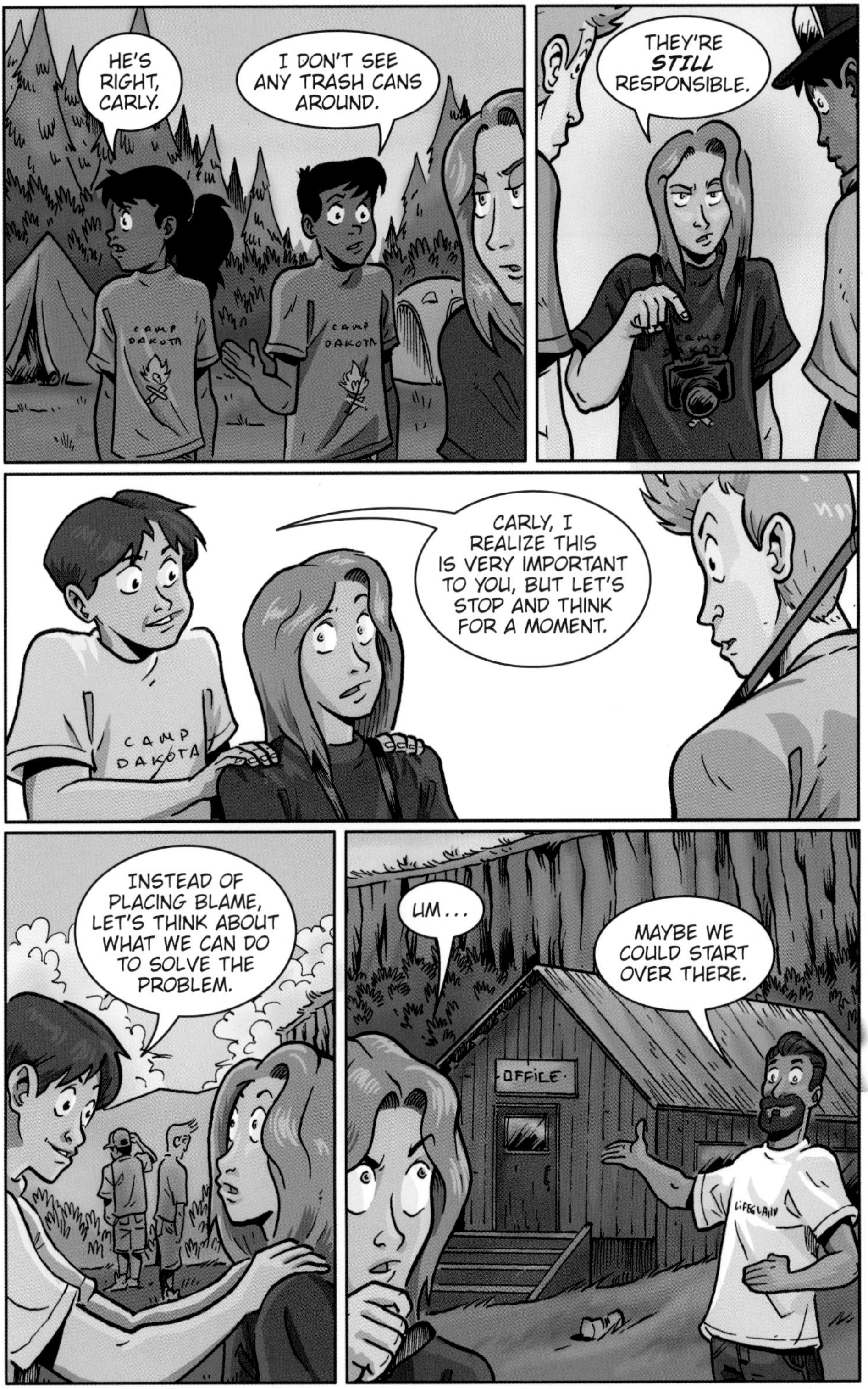
HE'S RIGHT, CARLY.
I DON'T SEE ANY TRASH CANS AROUND.
CAMP DAKOTA
THEY'RE *STILL* RESPONSIBLE.
CARLY, I REALIZE THIS IS VERY IMPORTANT TO YOU, BUT LET'S STOP AND THINK FOR A MOMENT.
INSTEAD OF PLACING BLAME, LET'S THINK ABOUT WHAT WE CAN DO TO SOLVE THE PROBLEM.
UM...
MAYBE WE COULD START OVER THERE.
OFFICE
LIFEGUARD

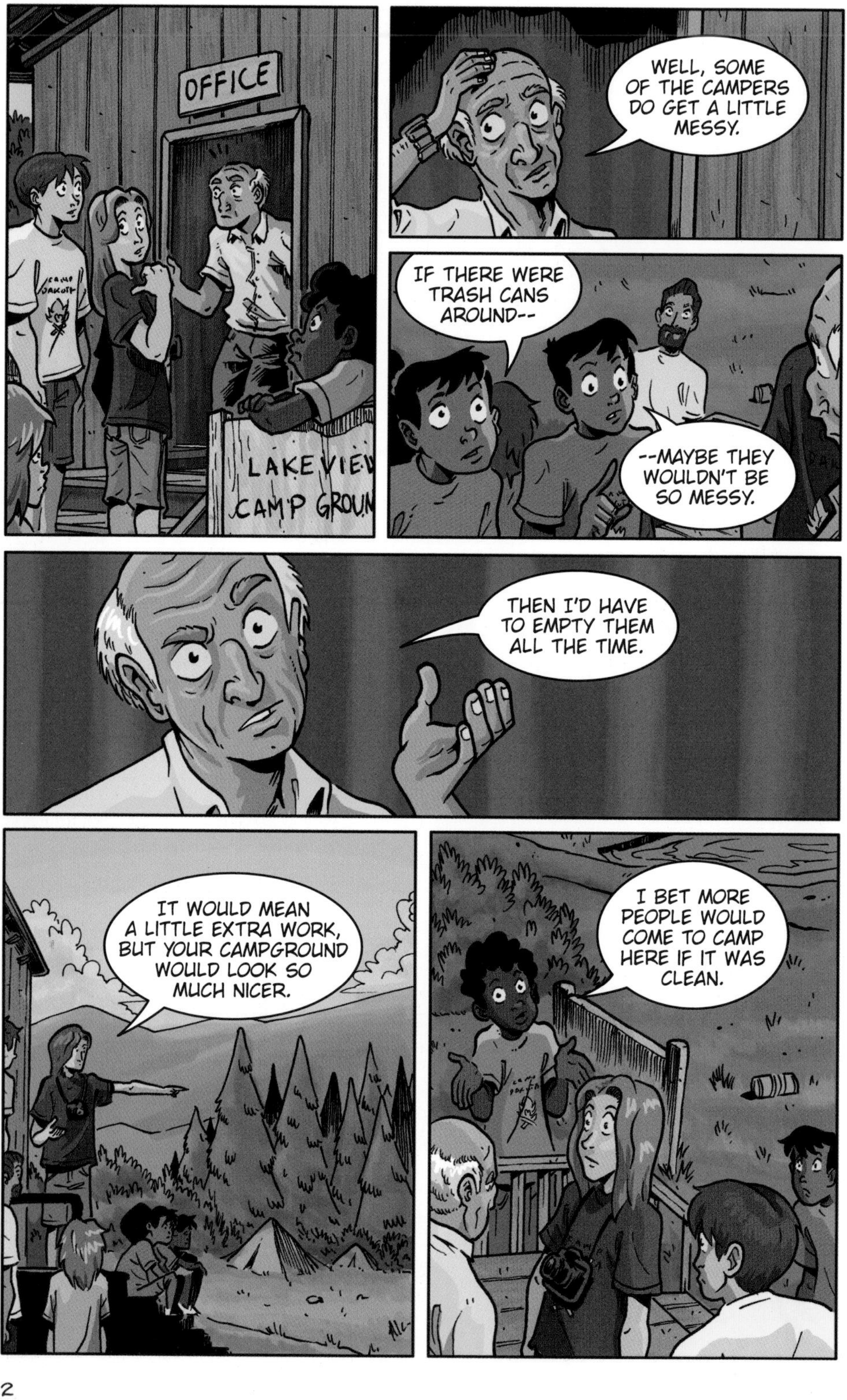
OFFICE
LAKEVIEW
CAMP GROUN
WELL, SOME OF THE CAMPERS DO GET A LITTLE MESSY.
IF THERE WERE TRASH CANS AROUND--
--MAYBE THEY WOULDN'T BE SO MESSY.
THEN I'D HAVE TO EMPTY THEM ALL THE TIME.
IT WOULD MEAN A LITTLE EXTRA WORK, BUT YOUR CAMPGROUND WOULD LOOK SO MUCH NICER.
I BET MORE PEOPLE WOULD COME TO CAMP HERE IF IT WAS CLEAN.

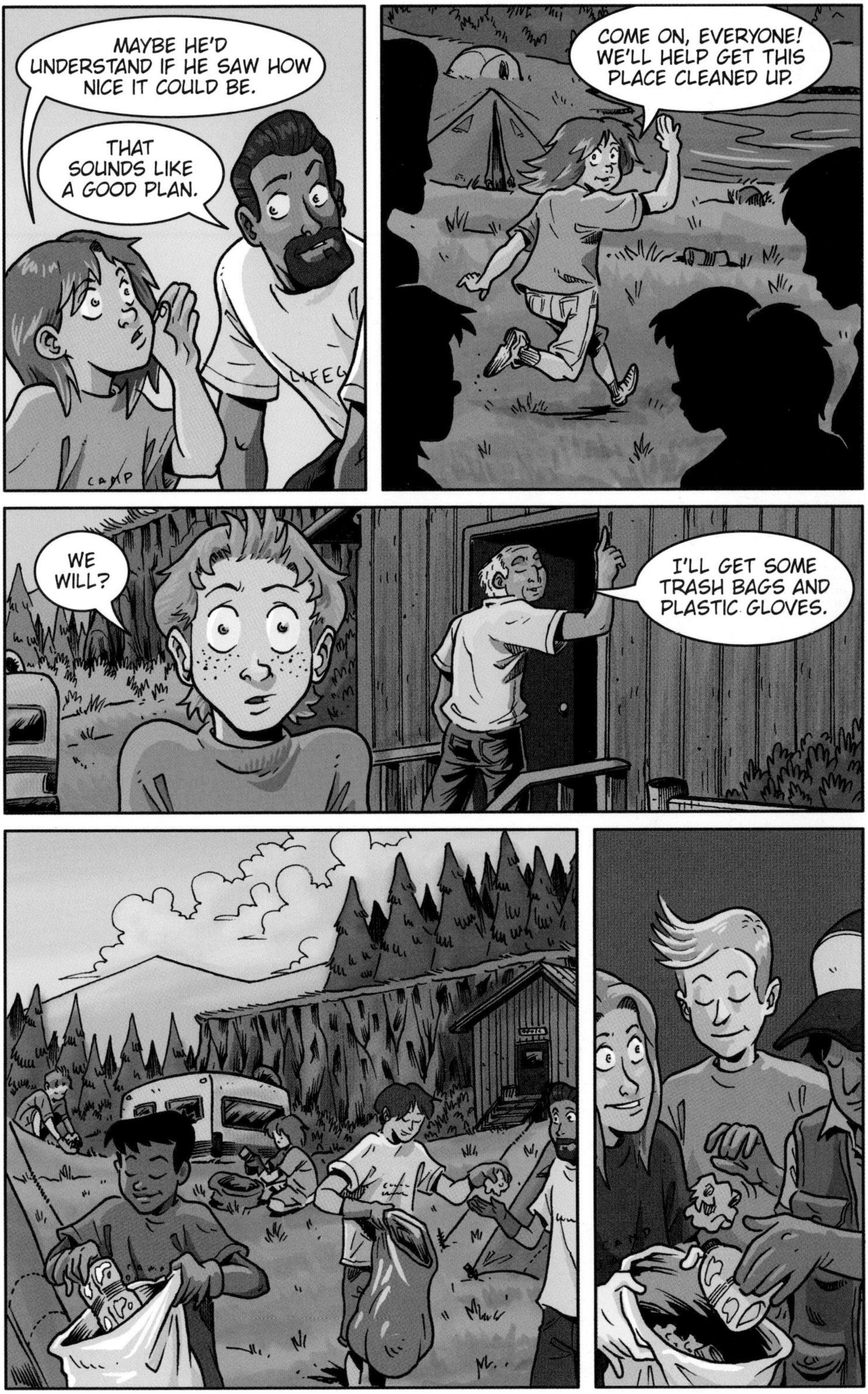
MAYBE HE'D UNDERSTAND IF HE SAW HOW NICE IT COULD BE.
THAT SOUNDS LIKE A GOOD PLAN.
COME ON, EVERYONE! WE'LL HELP GET THIS PLACE CLEANED UP.
WE WILL?
I'LL GET SOME TRASH BAGS AND PLASTIC GLOVES.

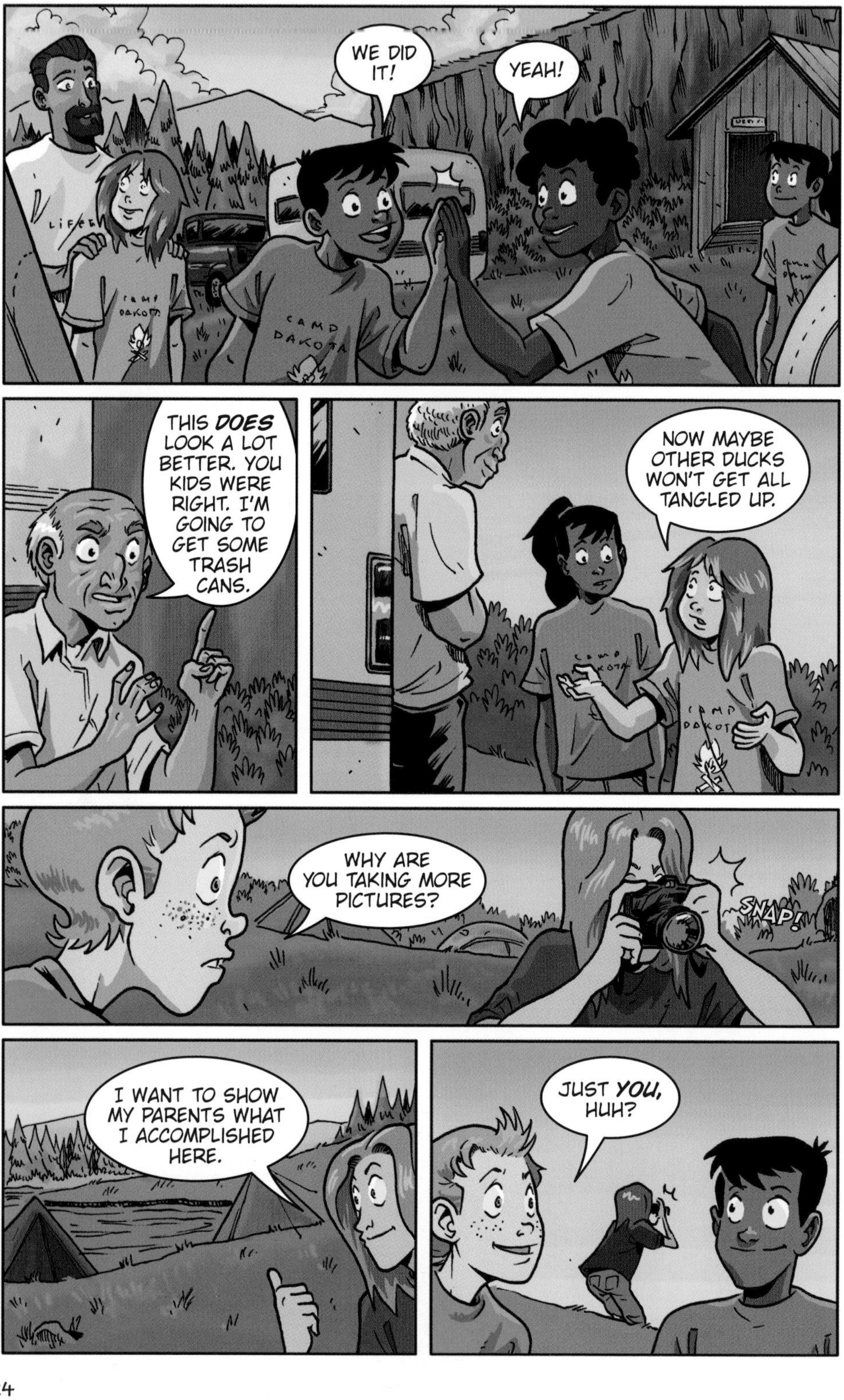
WE DID IT!
YEAH!
THIS DOES LOOK A LOT BETTER. YOU KIDS WERE RIGHT. I'M GOING TO GET SOME TRASH CANS.
NOW MAYBE OTHER DUCKS WON'T GET ALL TANGLED UP.
WHY ARE YOU TAKING MORE PICTURES?
SNAP!
I WANT TO SHOW MY PARENTS WHAT I ACCOMPLISHED HERE.
JUST YOU, HUH?

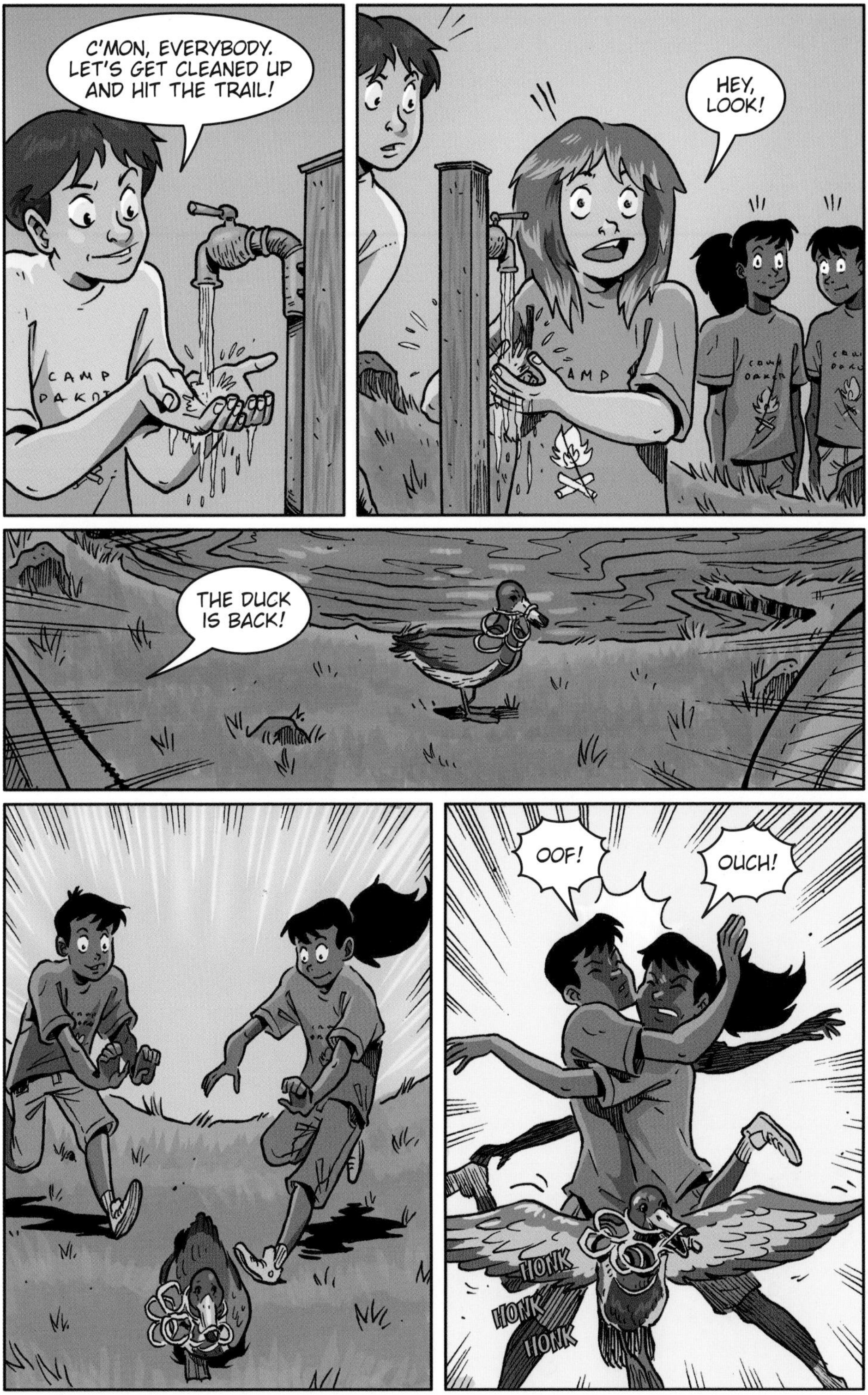
C'MON, EVERYBODY. LET'S GET CLEANED UP AND HIT THE TRAIL!
HEY, LOOK!
THE DUCK IS BACK!
OOF!
OUCH!
HONK
HONK
HONK

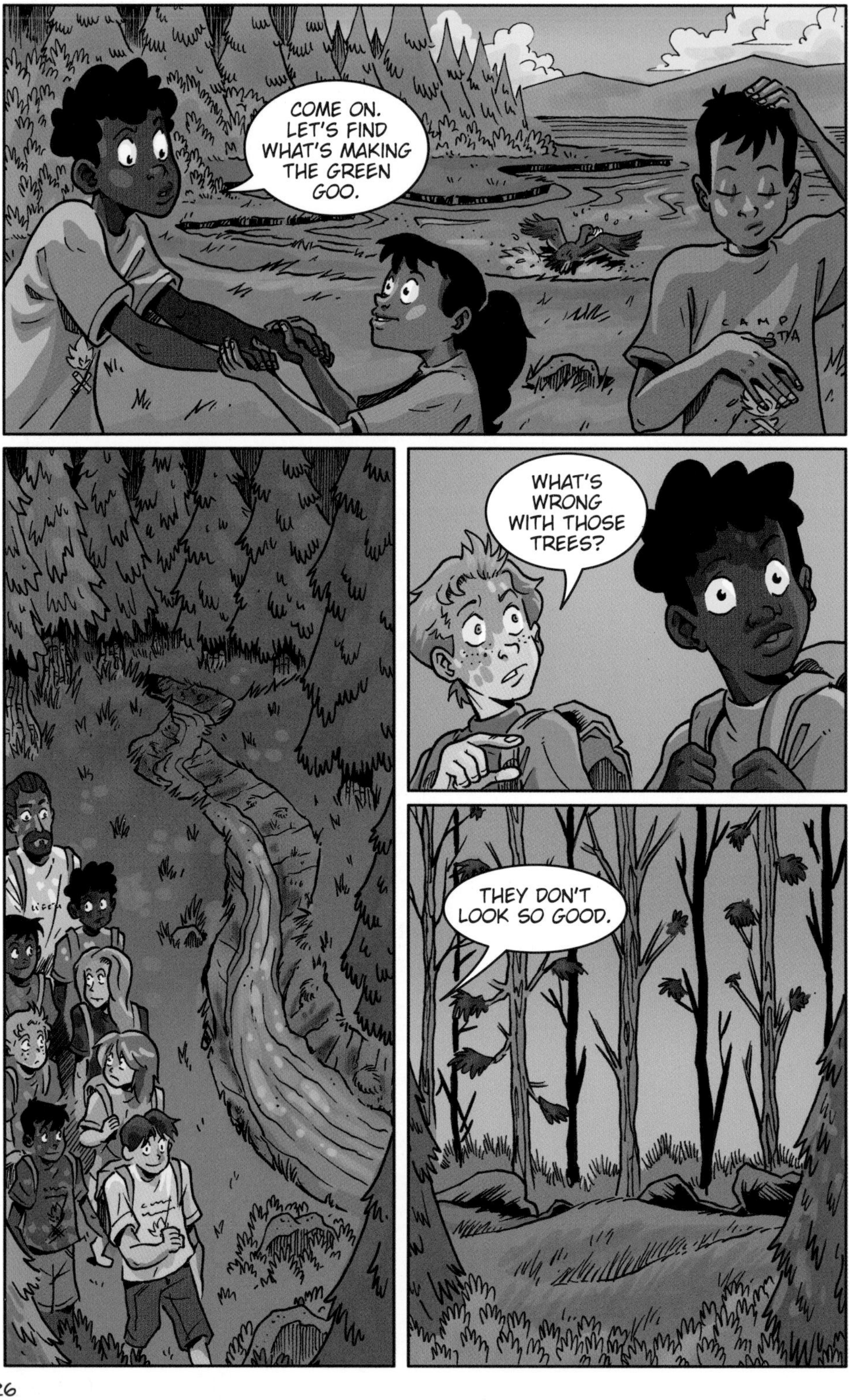
COME ON. LET'S FIND WHAT'S MAKING THE GREEN GOO.
WHAT'S WRONG WITH THOSE TREES?
THEY DON'T LOOK SO GOOD.

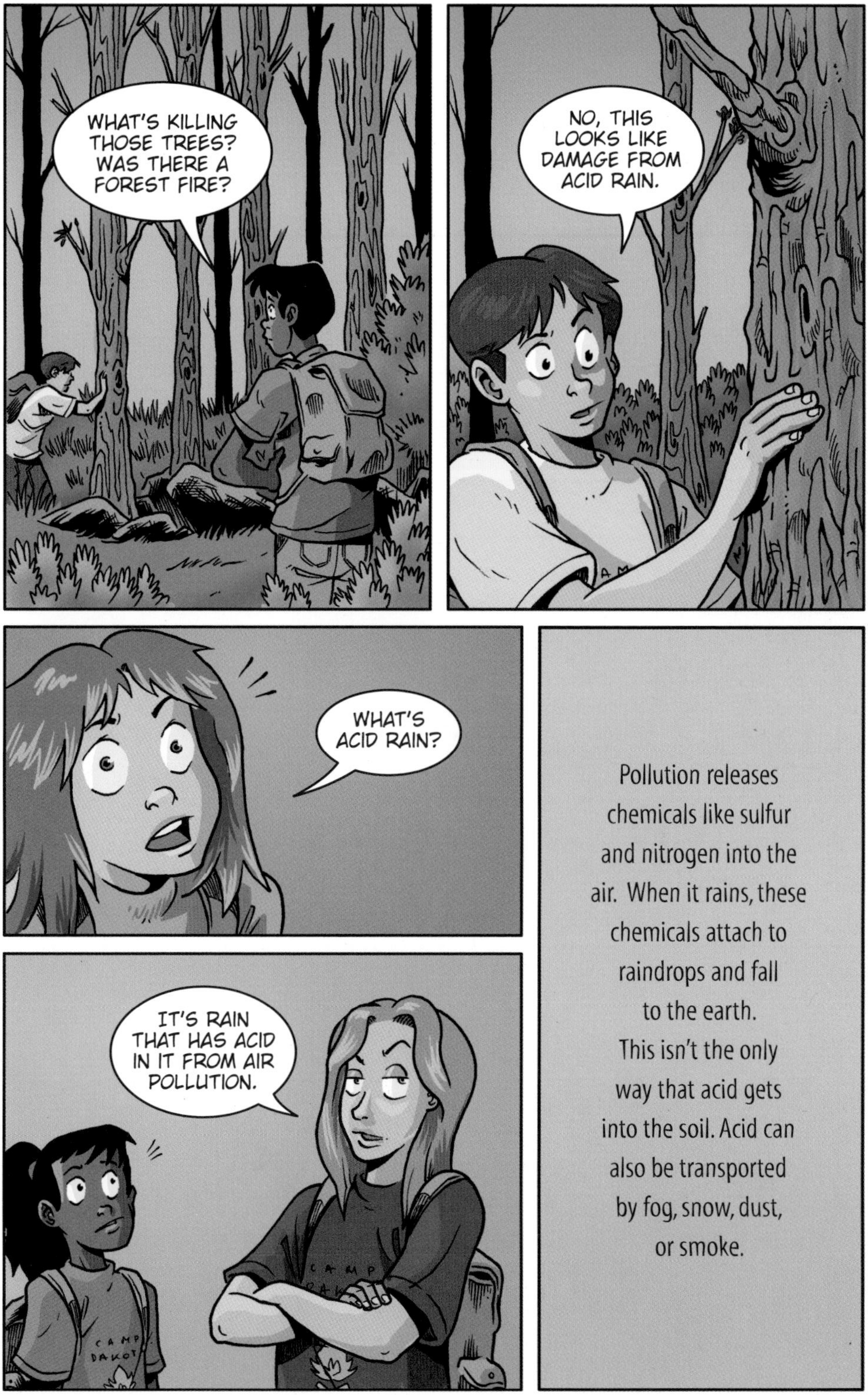
WHAT'S KILLING THOSE TREES? WAS THERE A FOREST FIRE?
NO, THIS LOOKS LIKE DAMAGE FROM ACID RAIN.
WHAT'S ACID RAIN?
Pollution releases chemicals like sulfur and nitrogen into the air. When it rains, these chemicals attach to raindrops and fall to the earth. This isn't the only way that acid gets into the soil. Acid can also be transported by fog, snow, dust, or smoke.
IT'S RAIN THAT HAS ACID IN IT FROM AIR POLLUTION.

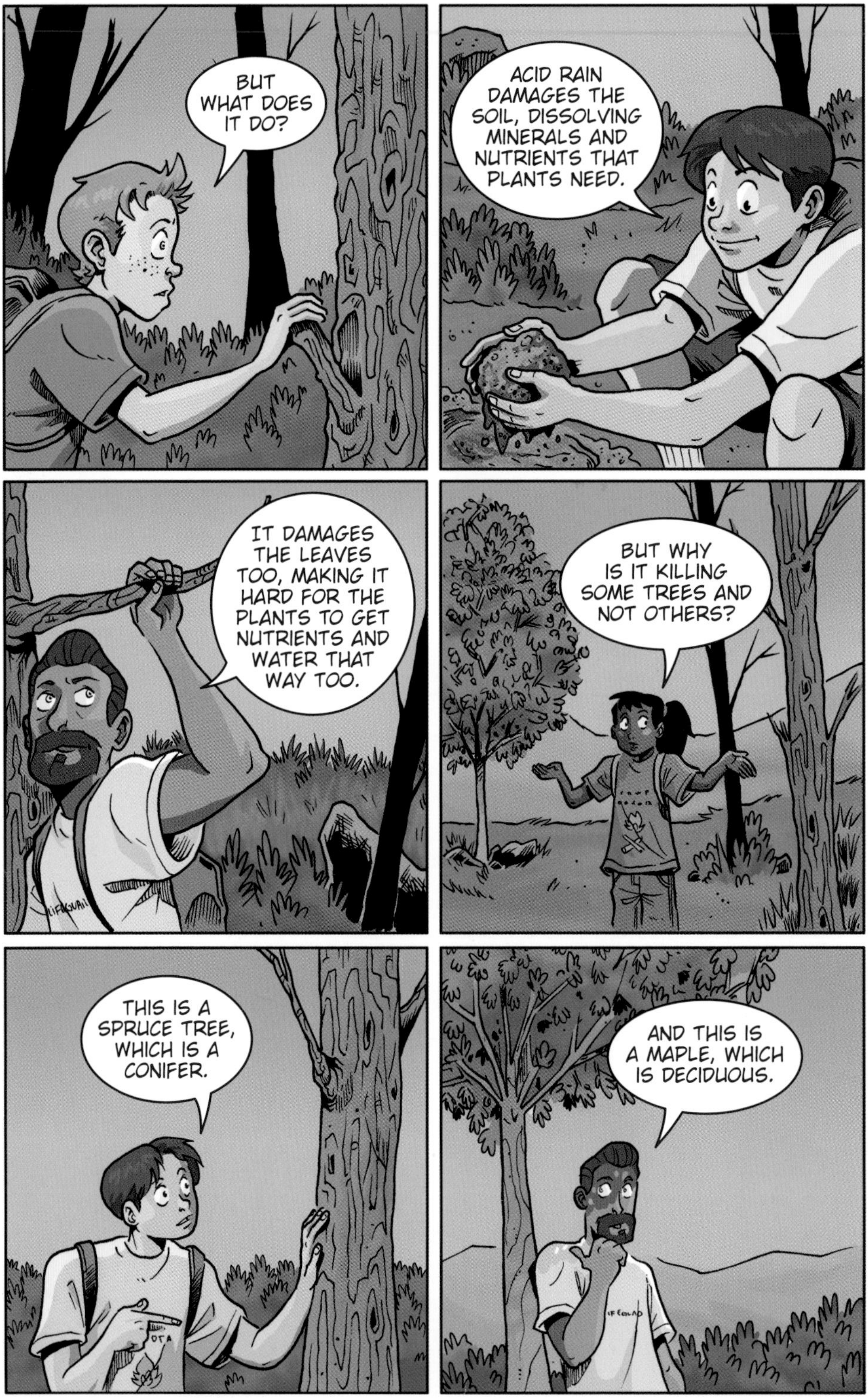
BUT WHAT DOES IT DO?
ACID RAIN DAMAGES THE SOIL, DISSOLVING MINERALS AND NUTRIENTS THAT PLANTS NEED.
IT DAMAGES THE LEAVES TOO, MAKING IT HARD FOR THE PLANTS TO GET NUTRIENTS AND WATER THAT WAY TOO.
BUT WHY IS IT KILLING SOME TREES AND NOT OTHERS?
THIS IS A SPRUCE TREE, WHICH IS A CONIFER.
AND THIS IS A MAPLE, WHICH IS DECIDUOUS.

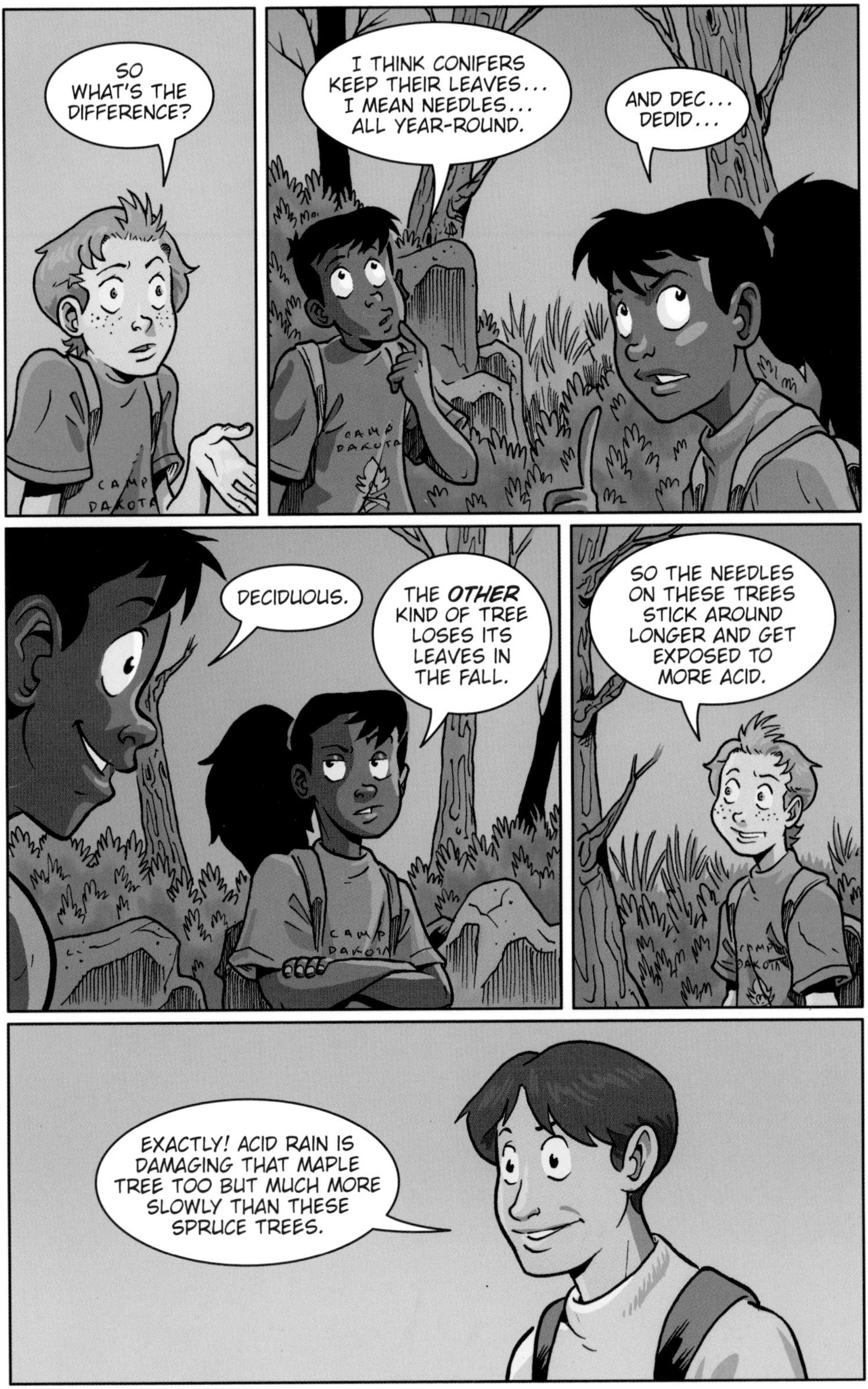
SO WHAT'S THE DIFFERENCE?
I THINK CONIFERS KEEP THEIR LEAVES... I MEAN NEEDLES... ALL YEAR-ROUND.
AND DEC... DEDID...
CAMP DAKOTA
DECIDUOUS.
THE *OTHER* KIND OF TREE LOSES ITS LEAVES IN THE FALL.
SO THE NEEDLES ON THESE TREES STICK AROUND LONGER AND GET EXPOSED TO MORE ACID.
EXACTLY! ACID RAIN IS DAMAGING THAT MAPLE TREE TOO BUT MUCH MORE SLOWLY THAN THESE SPRUCE TREES.

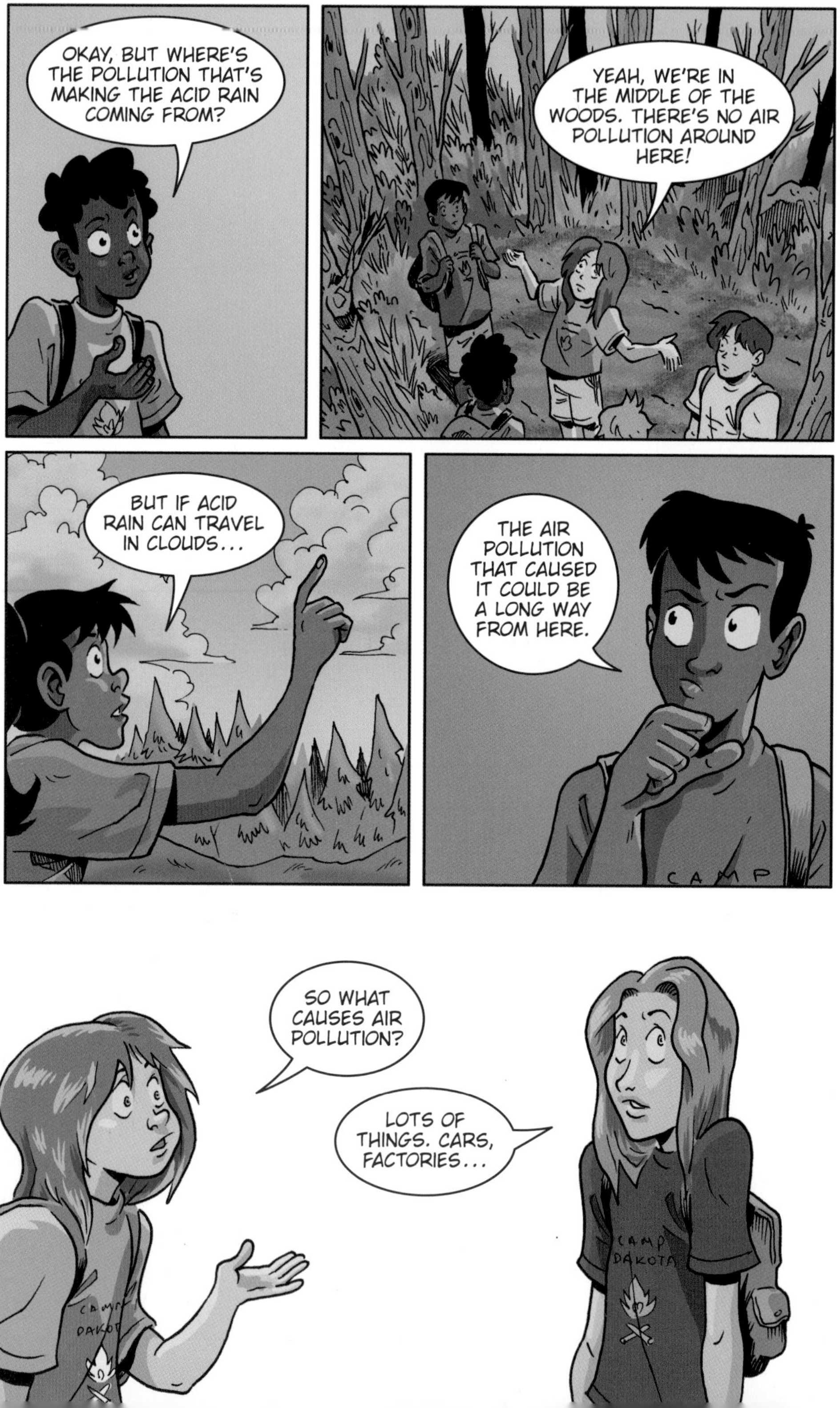
OKAY, BUT WHERE'S THE POLLUTION THAT'S MAKING THE ACID RAIN COMING FROM?
YEAH, WE'RE IN THE MIDDLE OF THE WOODS. THERE'S NO AIR POLLUTION AROUND HERE!
BUT IF ACID RAIN CAN TRAVEL IN CLOUDS...
THE AIR POLLUTION THAT CAUSED IT COULD BE A LONG WAY FROM HERE.
CAMP
SO WHAT CAUSES AIR POLLUTION?
LOTS OF THINGS. CARS, FACTORIES...
CAMP DAKOTA

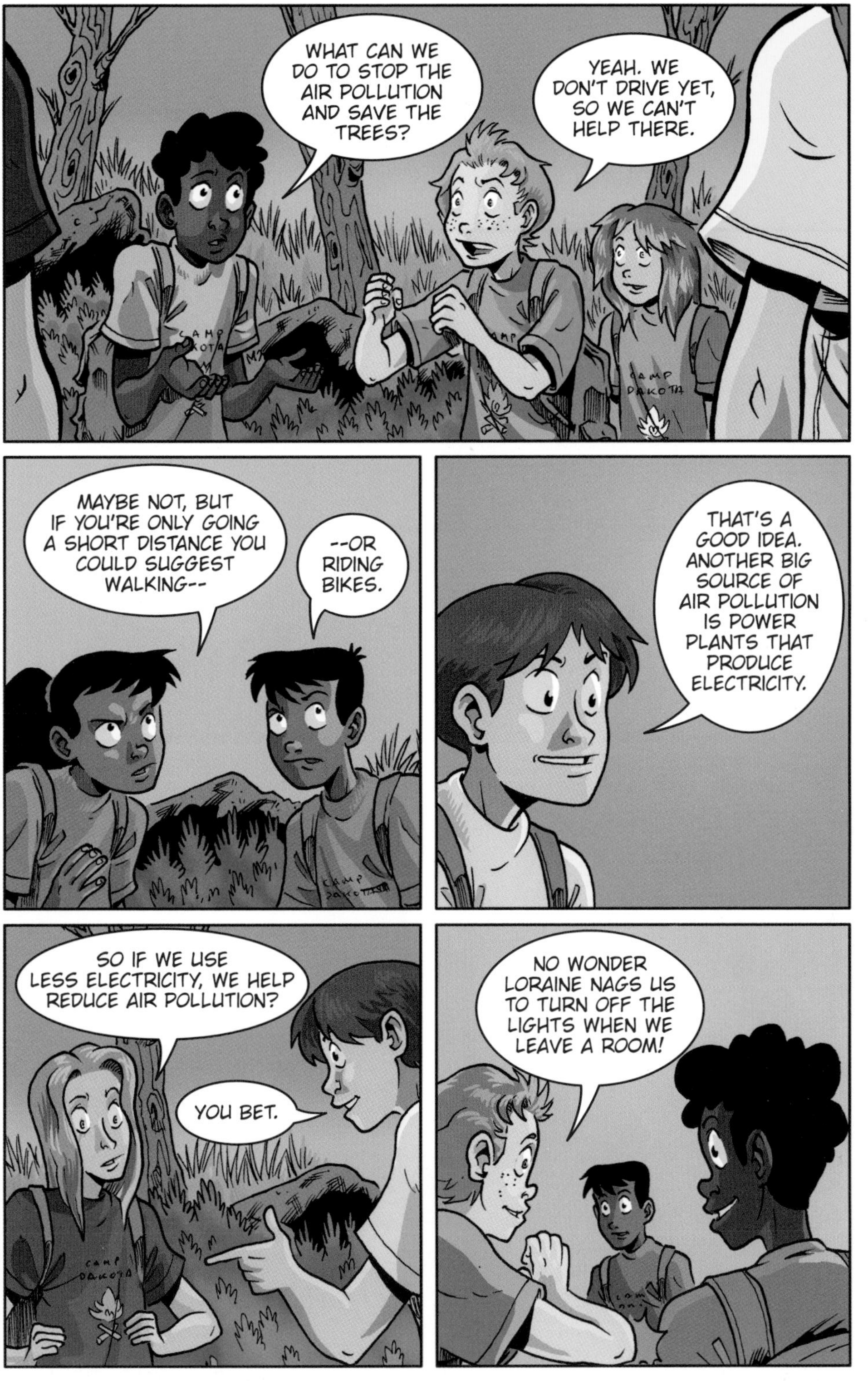
WHAT CAN WE DO TO STOP THE AIR POLLUTION AND SAVE THE TREES?
YEAH. WE DON'T DRIVE YET, SO WE CAN'T HELP THERE.
CAMP DAKOTA
MAYBE NOT, BUT IF YOU'RE ONLY GOING A SHORT DISTANCE YOU COULD SUGGEST WALKING--
--OR RIDING BIKES.
THAT'S A GOOD IDEA. ANOTHER BIG SOURCE OF AIR POLLUTION IS POWER PLANTS THAT PRODUCE ELECTRICITY.
SO IF WE USE LESS ELECTRICITY, WE HELP REDUCE AIR POLLUTION?
YOU BET.
NO WONDER LORAINE NAGS US TO TURN OFF THE LIGHTS WHEN WE LEAVE A ROOM!

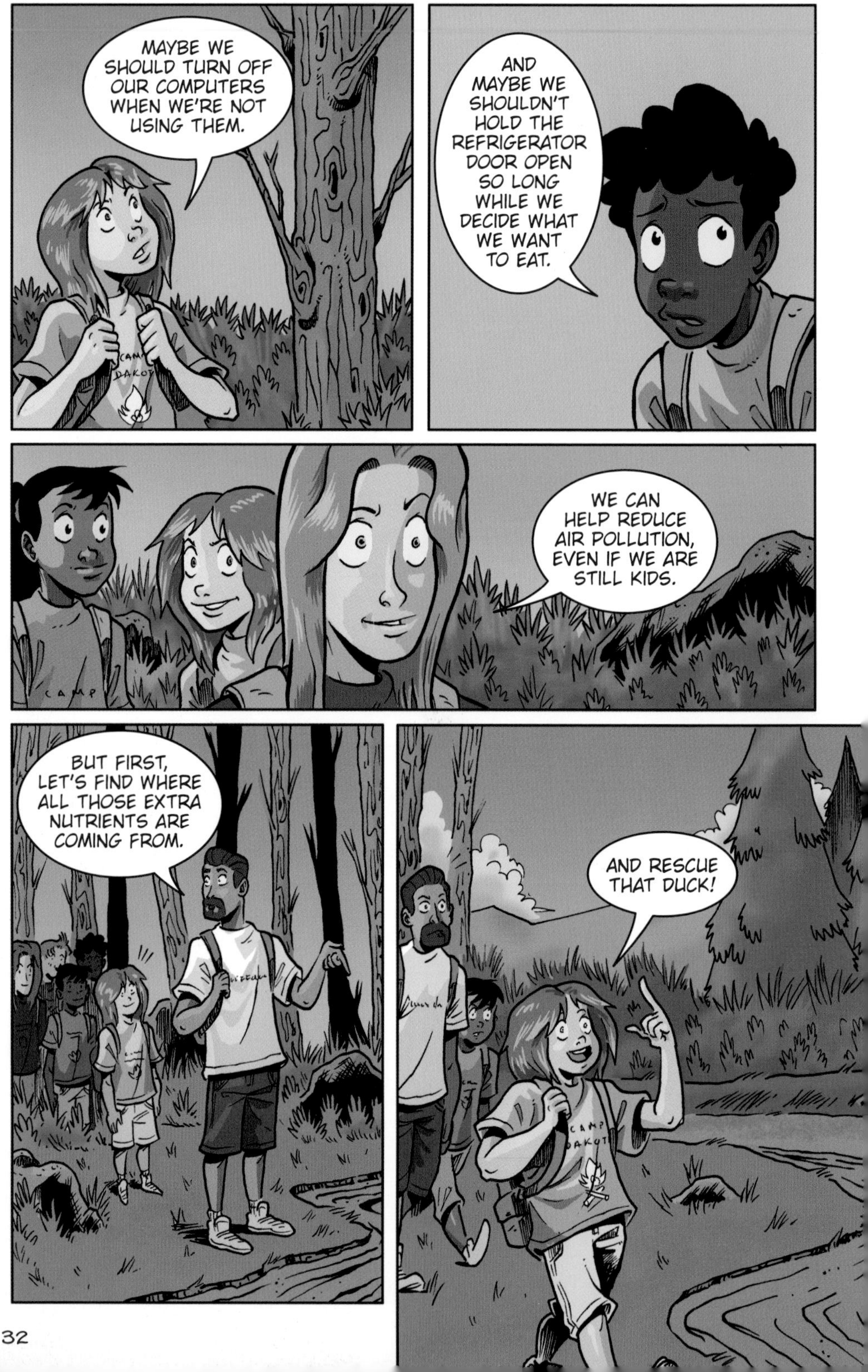
MAYBE WE SHOULD TURN OFF OUR COMPUTERS WHEN WE'RE NOT USING THEM.
AND MAYBE WE SHOULDN'T HOLD THE REFRIGERATOR DOOR OPEN SO LONG WHILE WE DECIDE WHAT WE WANT TO EAT.
WE CAN HELP REDUCE AIR POLLUTION, EVEN IF WE ARE STILL KIDS.
BUT FIRST, LET'S FIND WHERE ALL THOSE EXTRA NUTRIENTS ARE COMING FROM.
AND RESCUE THAT DUCK!

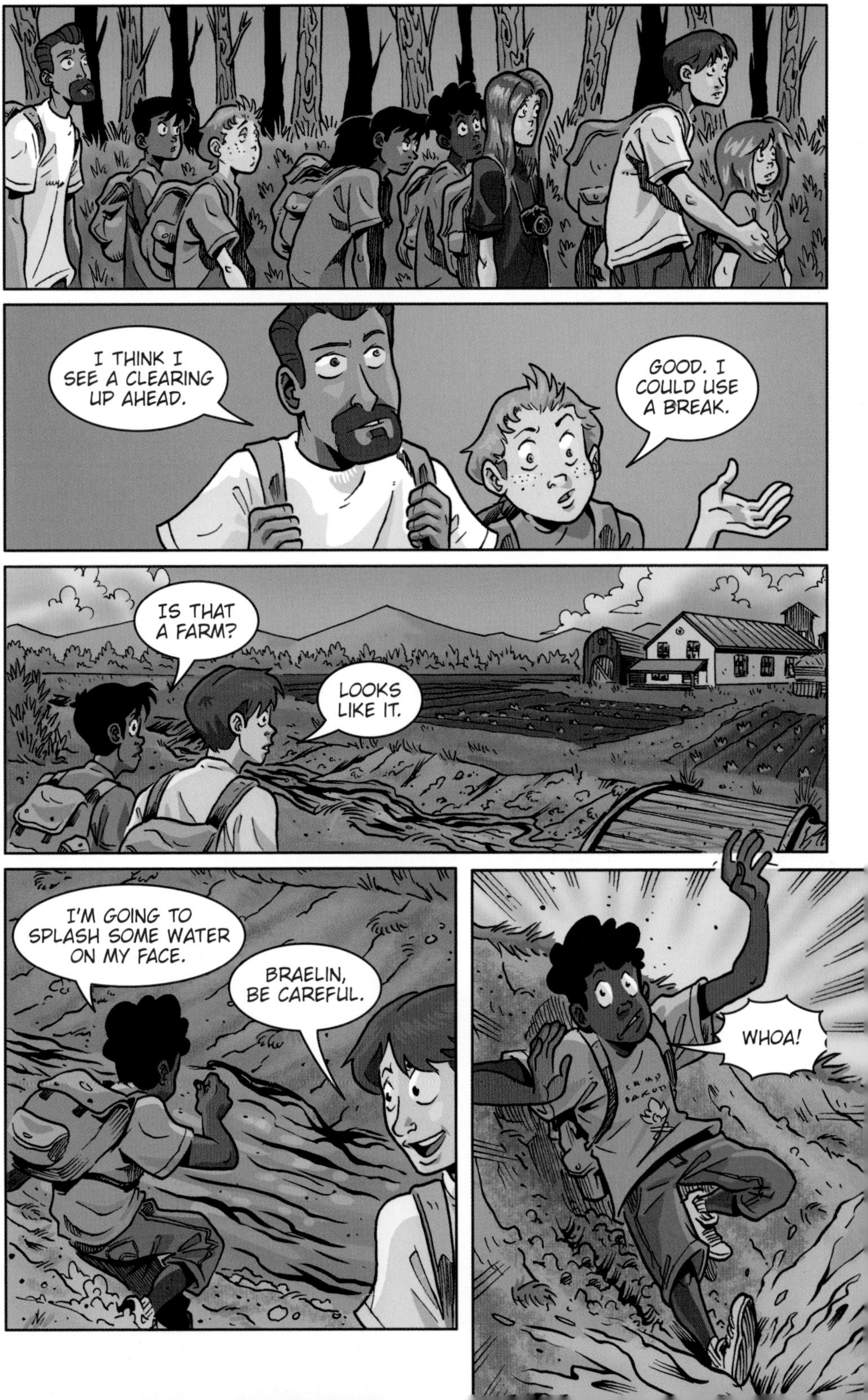
I THINK I SEE A CLEARING UP AHEAD.
GOOD. I COULD USE A BREAK.
IS THAT A FARM?
LOOKS LIKE IT.
I'M GOING TO SPLASH SOME WATER ON MY FACE.
BRAELIN, BE CAREFUL.
WHOA!

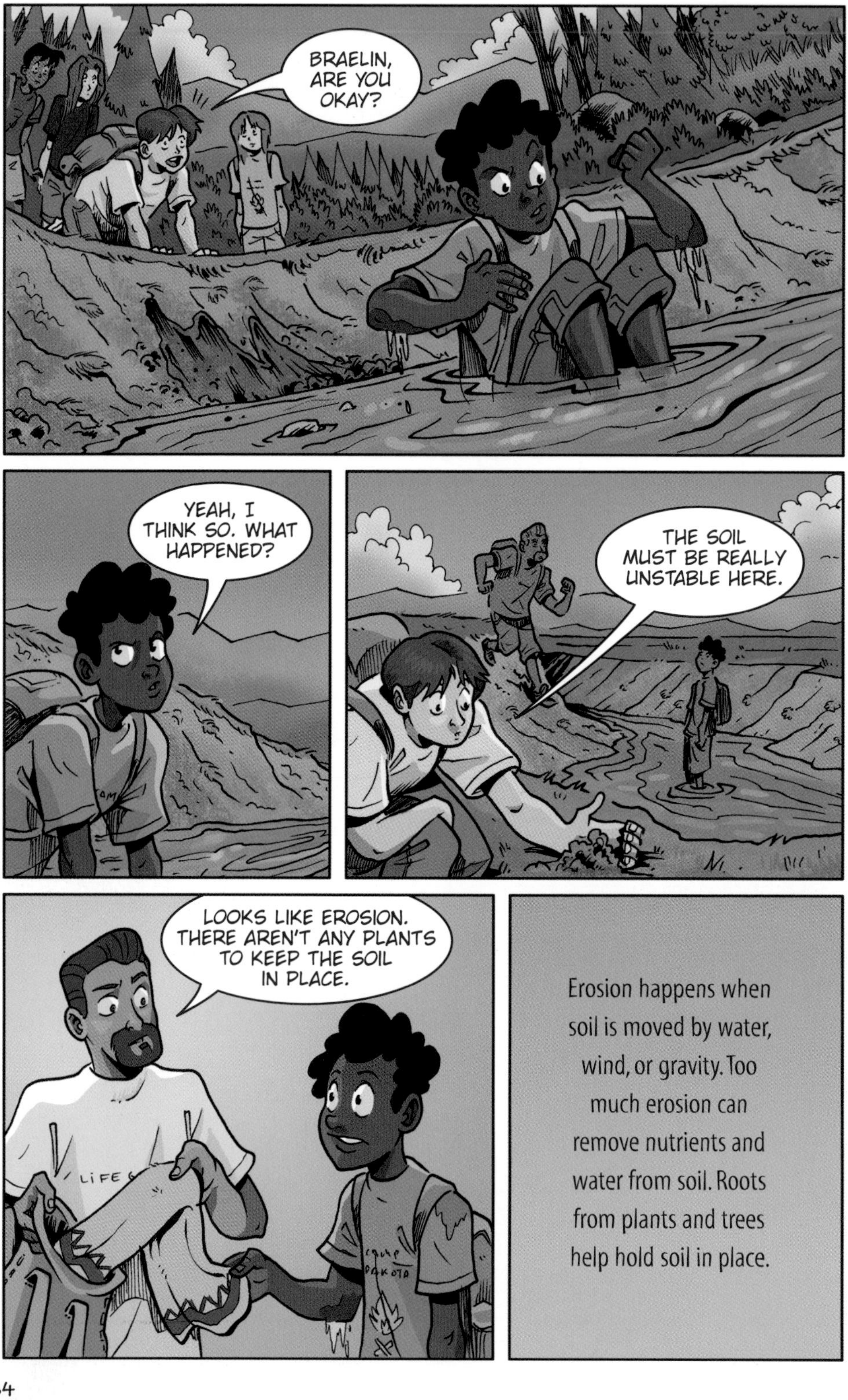
BRAELIN, ARE YOU OKAY?
YEAH, I THINK SO. WHAT HAPPENED?
THE SOIL MUST BE REALLY UNSTABLE HERE.
LOOKS LIKE EROSION. THERE AREN'T ANY PLANTS TO KEEP THE SOIL IN PLACE.
Erosion happens when soil is moved by water, wind, or gravity. Too much erosion can remove nutrients and water from soil. Roots from plants and trees help hold soil in place.

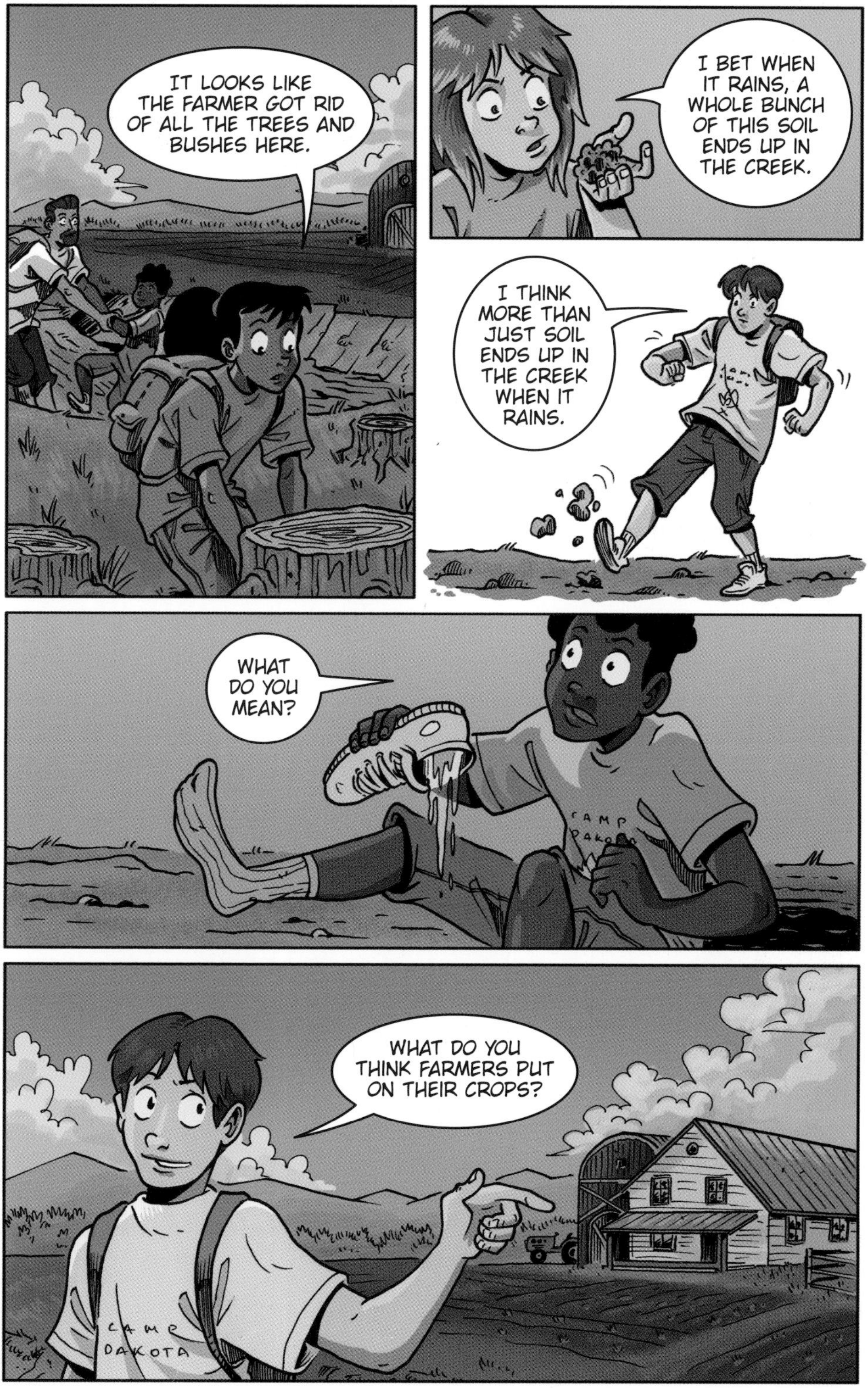
IT LOOKS LIKE THE FARMER GOT RID OF ALL THE TREES AND BUSHES HERE.
I BET WHEN IT RAINS, A WHOLE BUNCH OF THIS SOIL ENDS UP IN THE CREEK.
I THINK MORE THAN JUST SOIL ENDS UP IN THE CREEK WHEN IT RAINS.
WHAT DO YOU MEAN?
WHAT DO YOU THINK FARMERS PUT ON THEIR CROPS?
CAMP DAKOTA

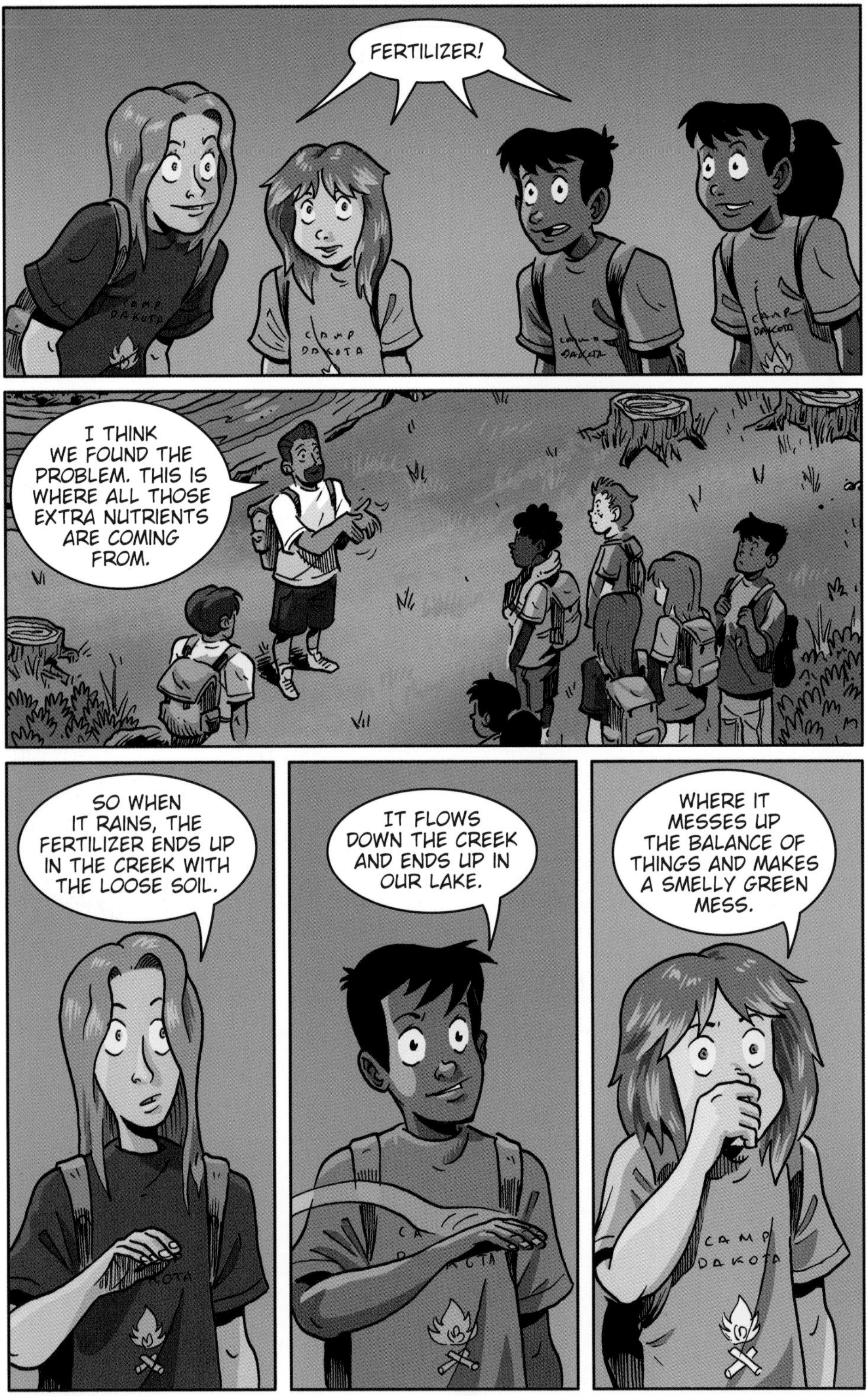
FERTILIZER!
CAMP DAKOTA
I THINK WE FOUND THE PROBLEM. THIS IS WHERE ALL THOSE EXTRA NUTRIENTS ARE COMING FROM.
SO WHEN IT RAINS, THE FERTILIZER ENDS UP IN THE CREEK WITH THE LOOSE SOIL.
IT FLOWS DOWN THE CREEK AND ENDS UP IN OUR LAKE.
WHERE IT MESSES UP THE BALANCE OF THINGS AND MAKES A SMELLY GREEN MESS.
CAMP DAKOTA

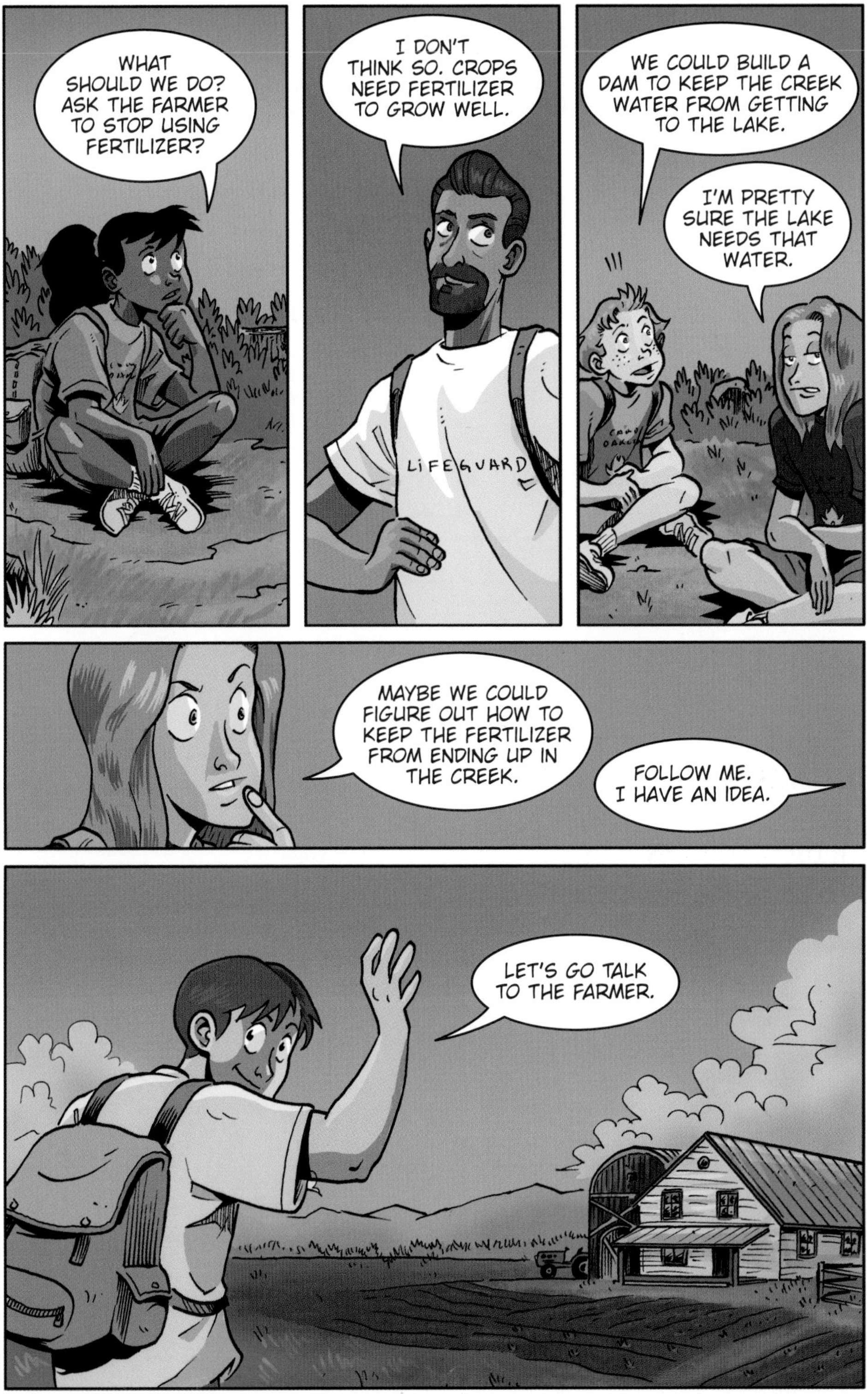
WHAT SHOULD WE DO? ASK THE FARMER TO STOP USING FERTILIZER?
I DON'T THINK SO. CROPS NEED FERTILIZER TO GROW WELL.
LIFEGUARD
WE COULD BUILD A DAM TO KEEP THE CREEK WATER FROM GETTING TO THE LAKE.
I'M PRETTY SURE THE LAKE NEEDS THAT WATER.
MAYBE WE COULD FIGURE OUT HOW TO KEEP THE FERTILIZER FROM ENDING UP IN THE CREEK.
FOLLOW ME. I HAVE AN IDEA.
LET'S GO TALK TO THE FARMER.

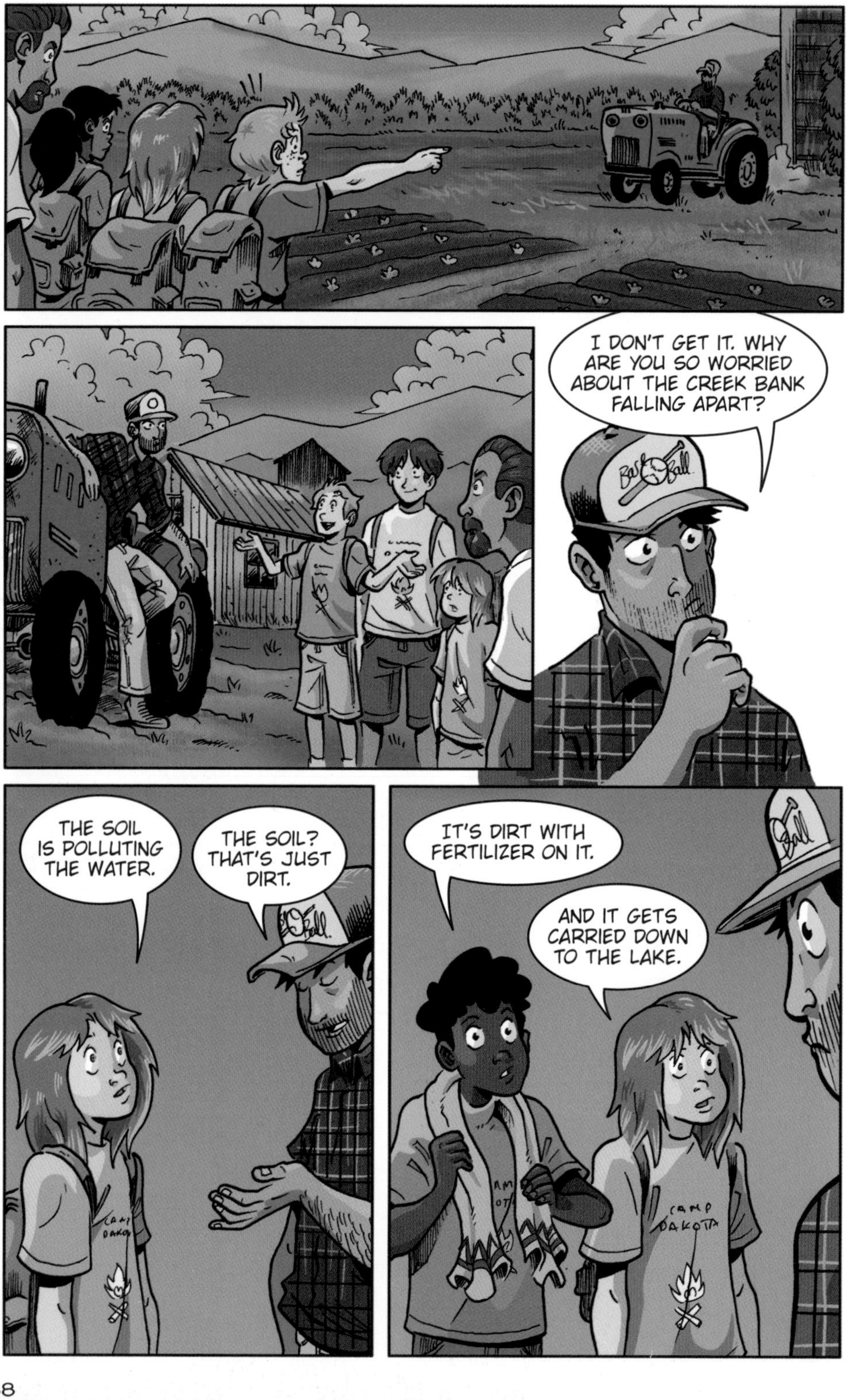

I DON'T GET IT. WHY ARE YOU SO WORRIED ABOUT THE CREEK BANK FALLING APART?
THE SOIL IS POLLUTING THE WATER.
THE SOIL? THAT'S JUST DIRT.
IT'S DIRT WITH FERTILIZER ON IT.
AND IT GETS CARRIED DOWN TO THE LAKE.

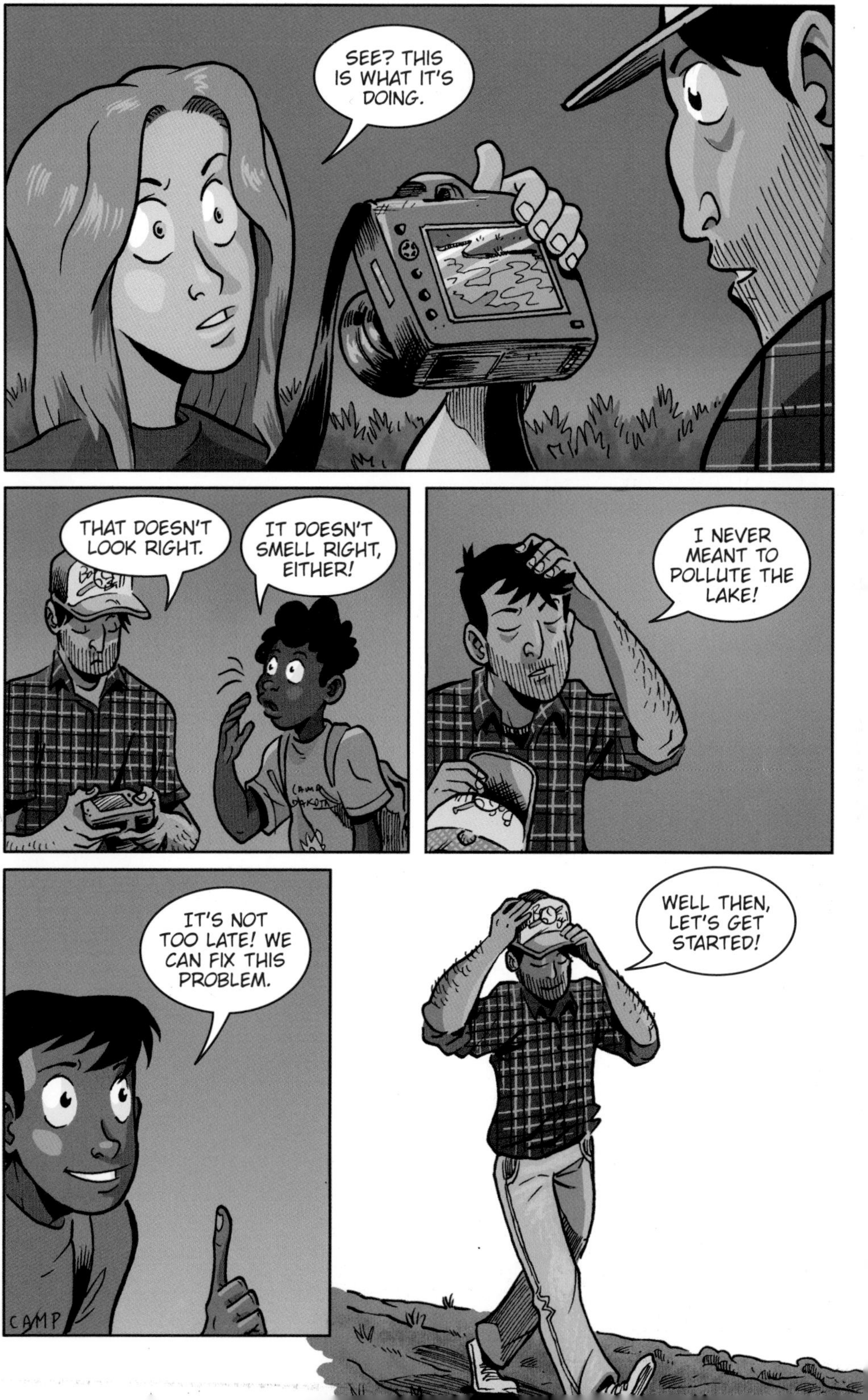
SEE? THIS IS WHAT IT'S DOING.
THAT DOESN'T LOOK RIGHT.
IT DOESN'T SMELL RIGHT, EITHER!
I NEVER MEANT TO POLLUTE THE LAKE!
IT'S NOT TOO LATE! WE CAN FIX THIS PROBLEM.
CAMP
WELL THEN, LET'S GET STARTED!

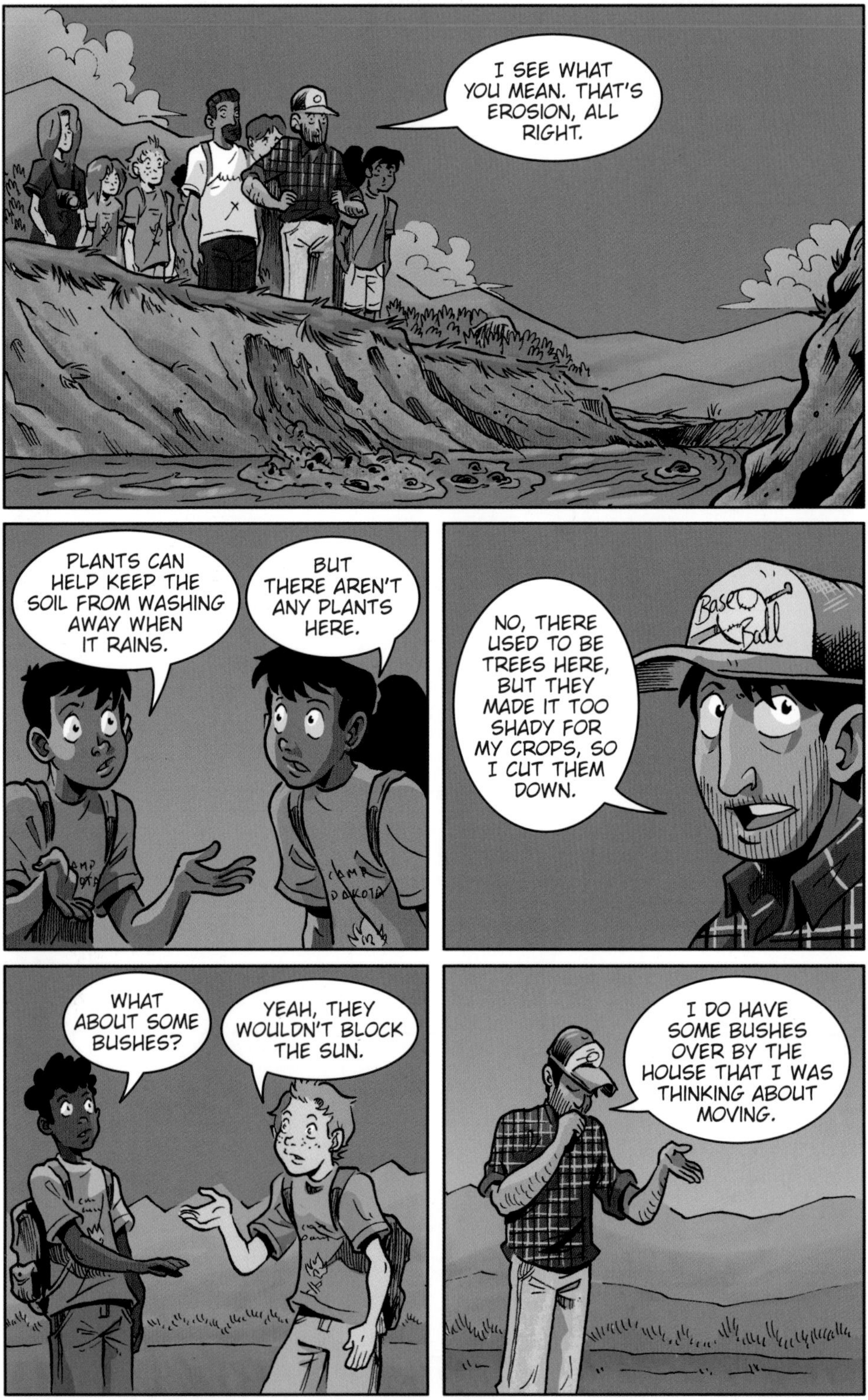
I SEE WHAT YOU MEAN. THAT'S EROSION, ALL RIGHT.
PLANTS CAN HELP KEEP THE SOIL FROM WASHING AWAY WHEN IT RAINS.
BUT THERE AREN'T ANY PLANTS HERE.
NO, THERE USED TO BE TREES HERE, BUT THEY MADE IT TOO SHADY FOR MY CROPS, SO I CUT THEM DOWN.
WHAT ABOUT SOME BUSHES?
YEAH, THEY WOULDN'T BLOCK THE SUN.
I DO HAVE SOME BUSHES OVER BY THE HOUSE THAT I WAS THINKING ABOUT MOVING.

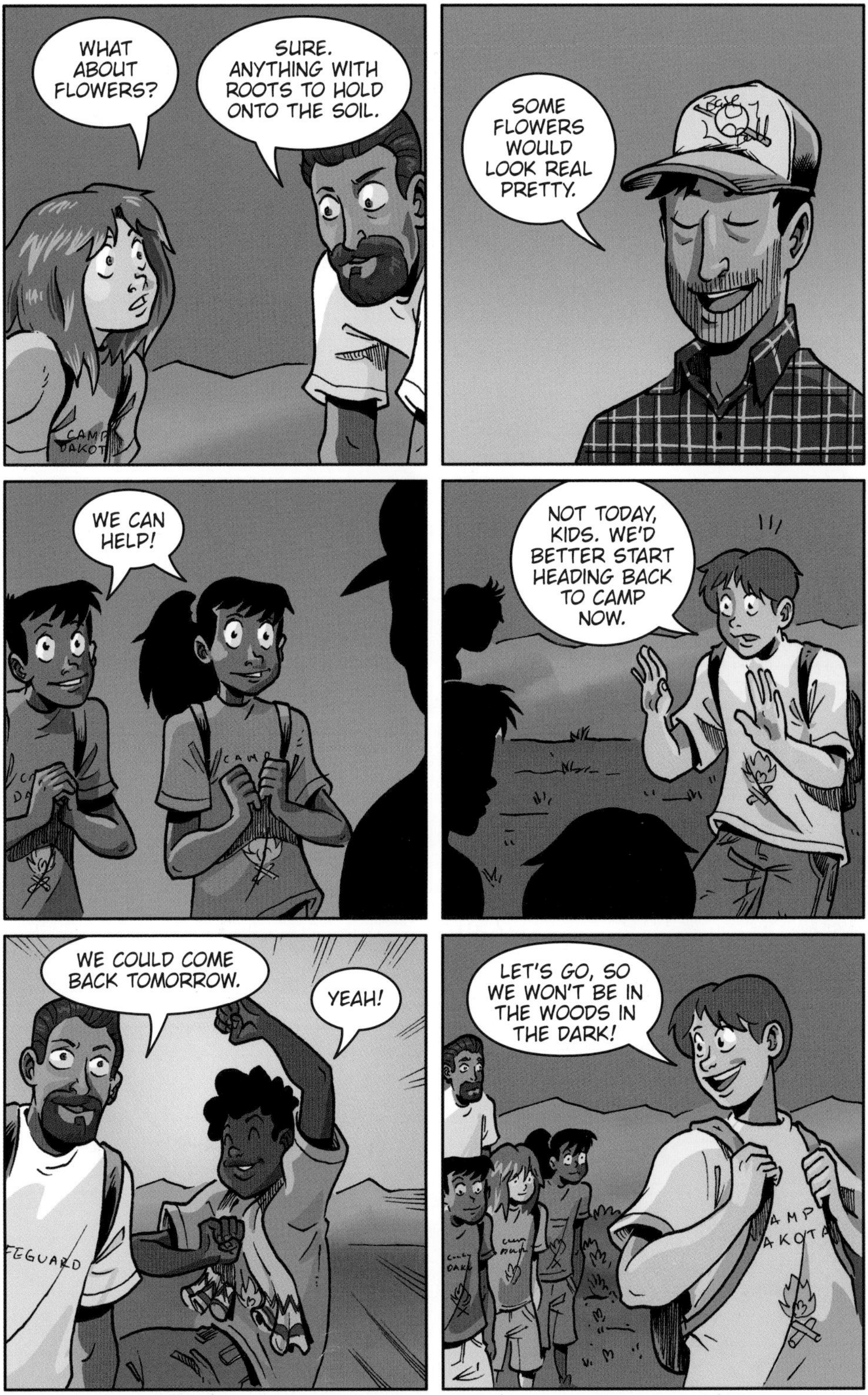
WHAT ABOUT FLOWERS?
SURE. ANYTHING WITH ROOTS TO HOLD ONTO THE SOIL.
SOME FLOWERS WOULD LOOK REAL PRETTY.
WE CAN HELP!
NOT TODAY, KIDS. WE'D BETTER START HEADING BACK TO CAMP NOW.
WE COULD COME BACK TOMORROW.
YEAH!
LET'S GO, SO WE WON'T BE IN THE WOODS IN THE DARK!

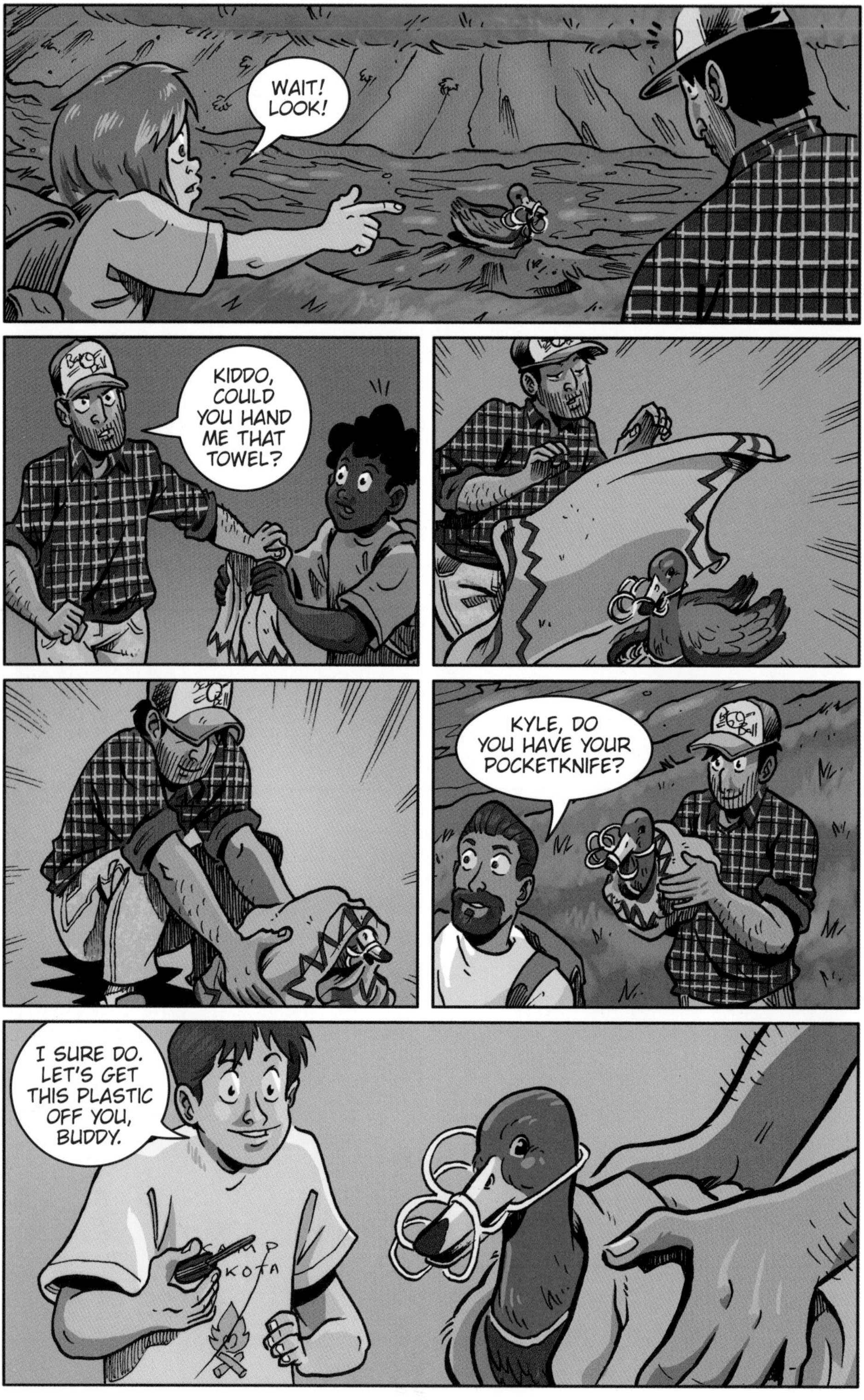
WAIT! LOOK!
KIDDO, COULD YOU HAND ME THAT TOWEL?
KYLE, DO YOU HAVE YOUR POCKETKNIFE?
I SURE DO. LET'S GET THIS PLASTIC OFF YOU, BUDDY.
CAMP KOTA

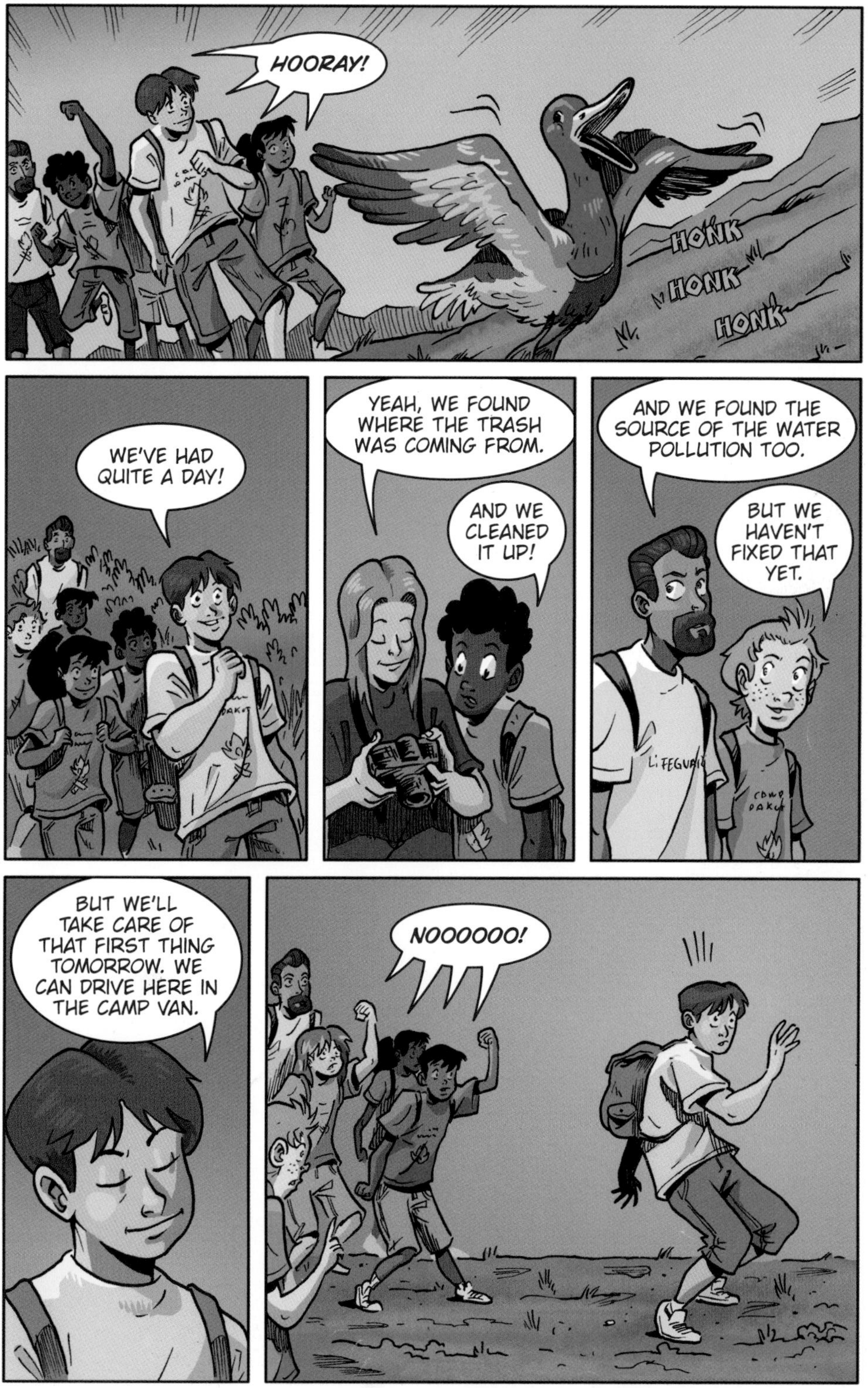
HOORAY!
HONK
HONK
HONK
WE'VE HAD QUITE A DAY!
YEAH, WE FOUND WHERE THE TRASH WAS COMING FROM.
AND WE CLEANED IT UP!
AND WE FOUND THE SOURCE OF THE WATER POLLUTION TOO.
BUT WE HAVEN'T FIXED THAT YET.
BUT WE'LL TAKE CARE OF THAT FIRST THING TOMORROW. WE CAN DRIVE HERE IN THE CAMP VAN.
NOOOOOO!

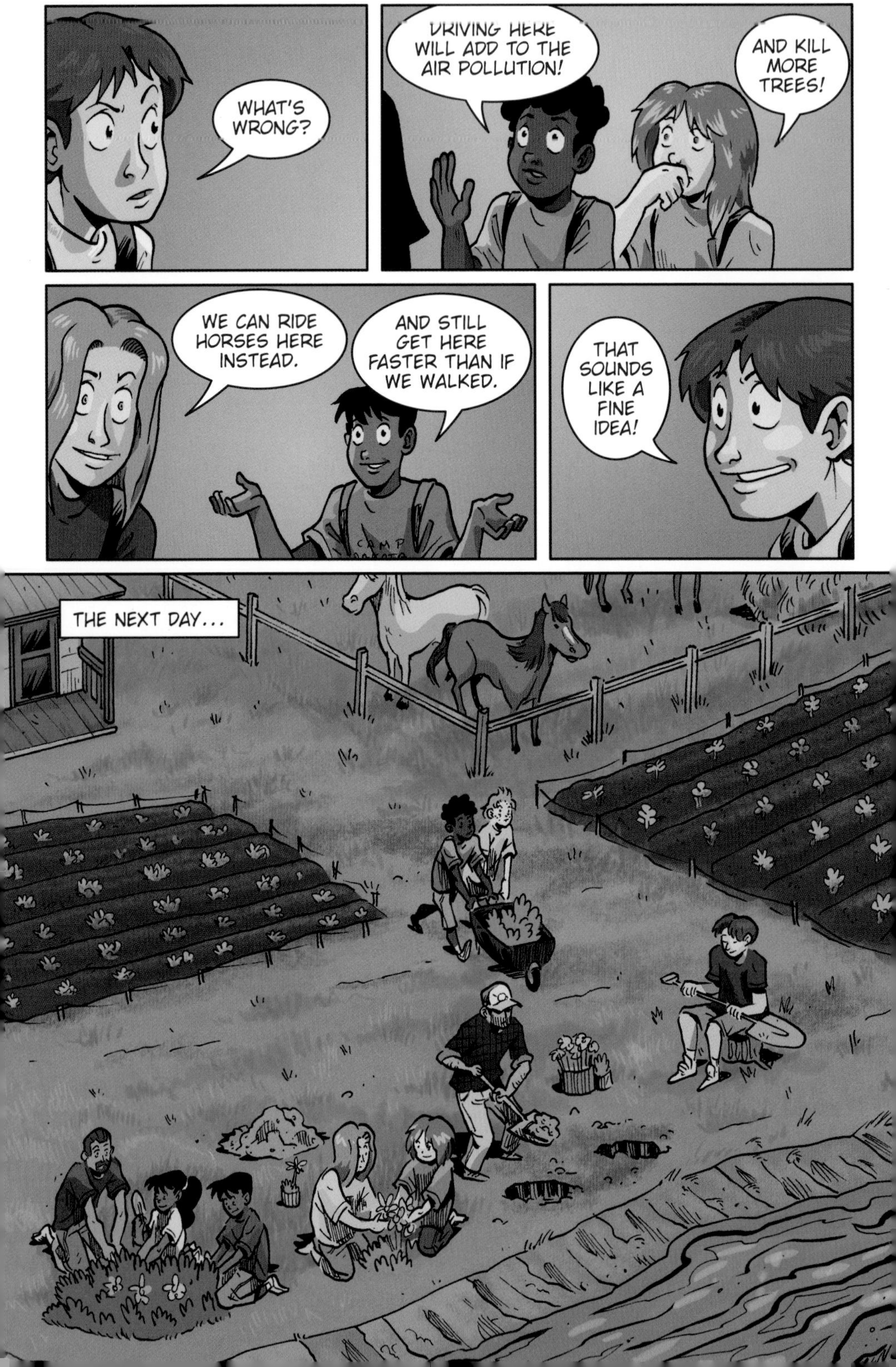
WHAT'S WRONG?
DRIVING HERE WILL ADD TO THE AIR POLLUTION!
AND KILL MORE TREES!
WE CAN RIDE HORSES HERE INSTEAD.
AND STILL GET HERE FASTER THAN IF WE WALKED.
THAT SOUNDS LIKE A FINE IDEA!
THE NEXT DAY...

# Experiments

Try these fun experiments at home or in your classroom.
Make sure you have an adult help you.

## Garbage Bag Ball and Chain

You will need: a large garbage bag with drawstring ties

1) Carry the garbage bag around with you all day. Put everything you throw away in it—scrap paper, water bottles, uneaten food, paper plates, juice boxes, plastic bags, facial tissues, and more.

2) At the end of the day, weigh the bag to see how much you threw away.

## What happened?

At the end of the day, you'll be tired of carrying that bag around, and it might not smell very good, either. Could you have recycled some of those items? Think about ways you can reduce the amount of trash you throw away on a daily basis.

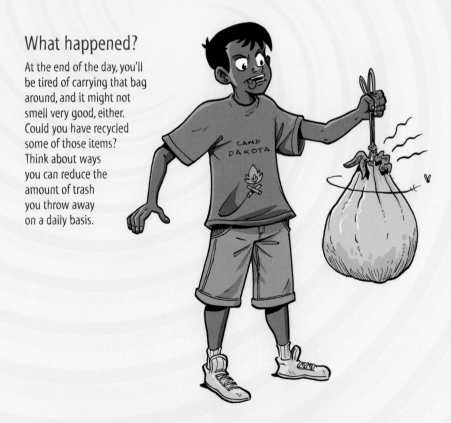

# Acid Rain Grass

What you will need: 2 small glass jars (baby-food size), measuring cup, masking tape, marker, vinegar, water, 2 clumps of grass, a notebook

1) Dig up 2 very small clumps of grass (make sure you ask an adult first). The clumps should have roots and dirt still attached.
2) Use the masking tape and the marker to label your jars "water" and "vinegar."
3) Put 1/8 cup water in one jar and 1/8 cup vinegar in the other. Make sure your labels match what you put in the jars.
4) Push a clump of grass down into each jar, so the roots and soil are mixing with liquid at the bottom.
5) Put the jars in a warm, sunny place for several days.
6) Write down observations in your notebook about what is happening to the grass samples every other day.

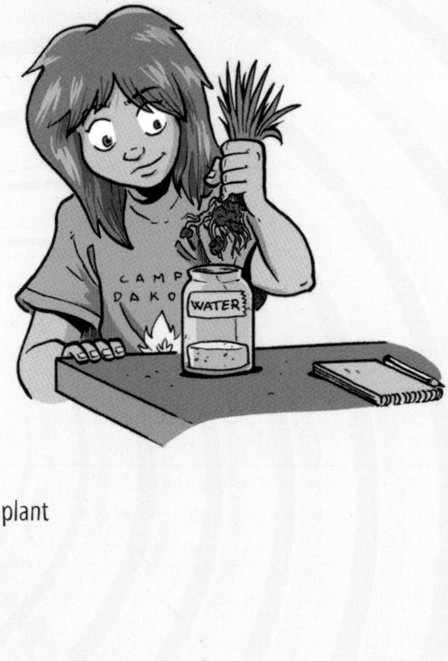
CAMP DAKO
WATER

## What happened?

Vinegar is an acid, so the grass reacted to it the way it reacts to acid rain. The damage starts where the acid touches it, then travels through the plant and slowly kills all of it, turning it brown.

The grass in the jar of water stayed green.

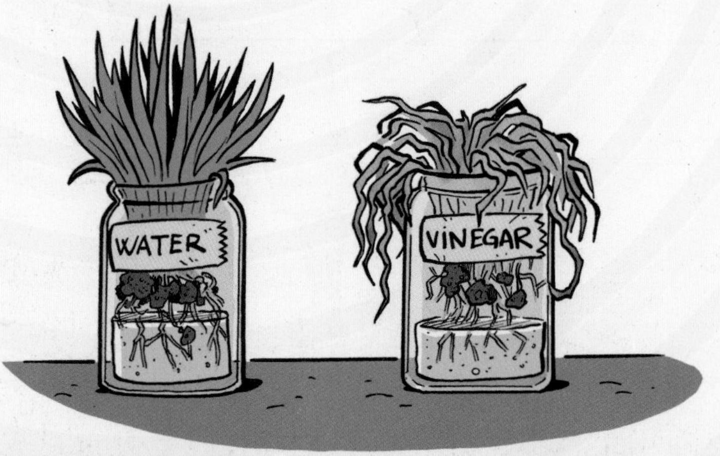
WATER
VINEGAR

# Mysterious Words

acid: a dangerous chemical

algae: a group of small water organisms that have no true roots, stems, or leaves

conifer: a tree or shrub that grows cones and has needles that stay green all year

deciduous: a tree or shrub that sheds its leaves every year

erosion: how the surface of the Earth is worn away by wind, water, or gravity

landfill: a low area of land where garbage is deposited

nitrogen: a colorless, odorless chemical that is found in fertilizer

nutrients: a substance that provides nourishment

plankton: a group of floating organisms in a body of water, usually made up of algae

pollutants: a substance that contains chemicals or waste products that are harmful to the air, soil, or water

pollution: the introduction of harmful substances to the environment

# Could YOU have solved the mystery of the Yucky Duck?

Good thing the kids of Camp Dakota knew a bit about pollution—and got some helpful tips from the counselors. See if you caught all the facts they put to use.

- Around the world, about seven million tons of plastic end up in the ocean. Beverage rings aren't the only problem. Wildlife can get tangled up in discarded fishing wire, and plastic bags can be mistaken for food by hungry sea turtles. You can help by encouraging your family to take reusable shopping bags with them when they head to the store.

- When extra nitrogen and phosphorus are present in lakes, algae grows quickly. Too much algae take away sunlight and oxygen from the plants and fish that need it. Soil erosion from farms is a common source of excess nitrogen and phosphorus.

- Wind can blow air pollution far away—it can travel over a hundred miles from its source. Air pollution can mix with water and return to the earth as acid rain. Acid rain damages a tree's leaves or needles. It can also damage soil by dissolving the nutrients plants need.

# THE AUTHOR

**LYNDA BEAUREGARD** wrote her first story when she was seven years old and hasn't stopped writing since. She also likes teaching kids how to swim, designing websites, directing race cars out onto the track, and throwing bouncy balls for her cat, Becca. She lives near Detroit, Michigan, with her two lovely daughters, who are doing their best to turn her hair gray.

# THE ARTIST

**GERMAN TORRES** has always loved to draw. He also likes to drive his van to the mountains and enjoy a little fresh air with his girlfriend and dogs. But what he really loves is traveling. He lives in a town near Barcelona, Spain, away from the noise of the city.